THE GUNSMITH

#5

THREE GUNS FOR GLORY

THE GUNSMITH

#5

THREE GUNS FOR GLORY

J.R. ROBERTS

SPEAKING VOLUMES, LLC

NAPLES, FLORIDA

2012

The GUNSMITH

#5 THREE GUNS FOR GLORY

ISBN 978-1-61232-608-5

Prologue

April, 1872

The two men following Wyatt Earp had every intention of robbing and killing him, but they had to wait until he picked up his money from the Caldwell Bank in Caldwell, Kansas.

"Seems to me we may be taking a long trip for nothing," complained Mike Gibson, the younger of the two men by three months. "What if he don't pick up no money?"

"Use your brain," said Jerry Martin, who was twenty-two years old. "Did you ever once see Earp spend any money? Aside from what he won from us in poker, I mean."

Gibson frowned, which he invariably did while thinking, because the process came unnaturally to him.

"No, can't say that I did," he finally answered.

"That means he must have been banking it the whole time," Martin reasoned. "I figure he's on his way to Caldwell to get his money from the bank. When he gets it, we'll get him. It's that simple."

"It always sounds simple when you explain it,"

Gibson told his friend, "but then something always goes wrong."

"Nothing is gonna go wrong if you do like I say, Mike."

"Sure, that's what you always say."

"And you always manage to fuck up," Martin reminded him. "If you'd leave the thinking to me and just do like I tell you, nothing would ever go wrong."

"You been telling me that since we was kids," Gibson complained.

"And you been fucking things up since we was kids," Martin added. "Now shut up and let me think."

Martin and Gibson had been friends ever since they were kids. Martin came from a rich family, and was the inevitable black sheep of his clan. His father and four older brothers never understood him, to hear him tell it, and when he turned nineteen he took his friend Gibson and struck out on his own.

Martin was built like a bull. He was about five-eight, but had a thick neck and round shoulders, and short but powerful legs. Gibson, on the other hand, was six-one and very thin. He was a follower and Martin was his leader. It was a situation he had accepted ever since he had first met Martin, when they were both five.

Up until a week ago they had been hunting buffalo with a group of men which included Wyatt Earp. While Martin and Gibson had spent their money as fast as they made it, Martin had observed that Earp rarely spent anything. For this reason, when the hunt broke up, Martin had decided to follow Earp and bushwhack him after he picked up his money. As they closed in on Caldwell, Kansas, Martin was sure they were getting closer and closer to Earp's money.

Earp had been the finest marksman on the hunt, which meant that he had made the most money.

"I still don't see why we don't just write to your Pa to send us some money when we run low. I know he'd do it," Gibson said.

"I know he'd do it, too," Martin told his friend, "but I don't want his money. Now shut up and let me think."

Gibson continued to grumble beneath his breath, but Martin was used to that and ignored it. He was busy trying to calculate how much money Wyatt Earp had saved up.

*   *   *

Wyatt Earp, 24 years old, was unaware of the two men trailing him to Caldwell, Kansas. He, too, was busy trying to calculate how much money was waiting for him in the bank there. He'd always made do with the small amounts he won playing poker, and had sent his pay on to Caldwell for safe-keeping until the end of the hunt. He did not want to be like the others, who, spending their money as fast as they made it, ended up broke when the hunt ended.

Wyatt remembered how his wife used to save as much as they could put aside, until she was taken from him by typhoid. He could still see her face and hear her voice, although she had been gone over a year.

He heard her telling him to save his money so

that they could buy themselves a little place some-day.

Since her death, his aims had changed some. The place he was now thinking of opening with his savings was a saloon and gambling house. His friend, Bartholomew, would be waiting for him in Caldwell with savings of his own; by combining their funds their dream could become a reality.

The two men on his trail, however, had their own dream, and the death of Wyatt Earp was a big part of it.

Chapter One

Kansas was beginning to wear thin on me, and the town of Caldwell did nothing to improve my impression.

Abilene had been, to say the least, unpleasant. My friend Bill Hickok had been marshall there, and had deputized me in an attempt to keep the lid on the town. When the final blow up came, however, the lid blew clean off and all hell broke loose. Bill had killed not only the town's most prominent gambler, Phil Coe, but one of his own deputies as well. A direct result of this confrontation was that gambling and the gamblers moved on from Abilene to Newton, and Bill Hickok moved on to only he knew where.

I had gotten as far as Newton, Kansas when illness felled my big black horse, Duke, forcing me to stay in that town for many more months than I had originally intended.

For a while it looked as if my big black buddy wouldn't make it, but finally he pulled through. Still, I had to wait until he had gained back most of the weight he lost and, he being such a big animal, that had also taken time.

During the wait I had lost track of Bill and had no idea where he was now, or what he was doing. I had become aware in Abilene that Bill had been having trouble with his eyes, which may have been the reason he had accidently gunned down his friend and deputy, Mike Williams. I had advised Bill to seek medical help, but he had been afraid that if the word got around that he was having problems with his eyes, he would become a target for every tinhorn gunslinger in the West. I couldn't argue with that, but I hoped that he had been able to find help without news getting around. Maybe that was why I hadn't heard anything about him since December '71.

It was now April '72, and Duke was able to travel. I had been working as a dealer in a small saloon owned by Ben Thompson, a gunman who had been Phil Coe's partner in Abilene. After Coe's death, Thompson had moved on to Newton and opened a smaller place. When I reached Newton and found out I'd be stuck there for a while, Thompson offered me a job, and I took it.

My last night in Newton had been spent in the company of a young lady named Karen, who also worked in Thompson's saloon. During my stay I had spread my attention among the female populace, but Karen was my favorite. And I explained that to her, also explaining that this was to be my last night in Newton. She had been only too willing to share it with me.

That morning I woke up with her red curls tickling my nostrils, and for some reason I woke up hard and ready for action. I reached over and grasped her soft buttocks in my hands, lifted her up and impaled her on my rigid shaft. Still half asleep, she moaned as I entered her and then I began to slide her up and down my erection. She was a small girl and I handled her with ease.

"Oh, God," she murmured, coming awake. "Oh, Jesus!"

She kissed me and continued to murmur into my mouth, which excited me even more, for some reason. I began to work her faster and faster until her breath was coming in short, ragged gasps and when we finally came it was together, a mutual explosion which lifted us both off the bed.

"Oh, my, Clint Adams," she told me after she caught her breath, "you are a special, special man."

"And you're a special lady," I replied.

"And you're still leaving," she told me.

"That's right," I told her.

She made a face and slid off me.

"Got time for breakfast?" she asked, standing next to the bed. Barely five feet tall, she had large breasts for a girl her size. They were firm and taut, with large nipples and wide aureolas.

I reached up and cupped one smooth, firm breast and said, "I thought I just had breakfast."

She slapped my hand away playfully and said, "I'll get you some eggs. You can't travel on an empty stomach."

After eggs and coffee—lots and lots of strong coffee—we said quick goodbyes and I went to see Thompson.

"Time for me to go, Ben," I told him.

"Take care, Clint," he said, handing me my final pay. "Did you say goodbye to Karen?"

"All night long," I answered. He laughed and we shook hands. Never the best of friends we nevertheless had mutual respect for each other. He did not hold anything that had happened in Abilene against me, because he felt that the confrontation between Bill Hickok and Phil Coe had been inevitable, whether I was there or not. Hiring me had been good business, because he'd needed a good dealer and I was available.

"Where are you heading now?" he asked.

"Out of Kansas," I told him.

"Can't say that I blame you. Good luck."

"Thanks, Ben."

I went to the livery, where the livery man had my rig and Duke all ready to go. As I rode out of Newton, my intention was to keep going until I was out of Kansas. Unfortunately, Caldwell, Kansas got in my way.

Chapter Two

Just outside of Caldwell, one of the horses in my team threw a shoe. I had planned to bypass the town of Caldwell completely, but I didn't want to chance injuring the horse, so I turned the team and headed into Caldwell.

"I got to finish a job I'm doing," the livery man told me. "Soon as I'm finished with that one, I can work on your horse."

It sounded fair, so I threw him a couple of extra dollars to feed Duke well, and went in search of a saloon.

As I approached the Caldwell saloon, I noticed a tall man pull his mount up in front and get off. I thought I recognized him, but I couldn't be sure. It had been over a year since I'd last seen him, and that had been the only time we ever met. We had only spoken for an hour or so, but he and Wild Bill had pulled my fat out of the fire that day, and you don't forget a man after he does that for you, especially when he don't know you from Adam.

He tied off his horse, removed his hat and pounded some of the trail dust from his clothes with it. Without his hat I was sure he was the man

I thought he was, and I walked up to him.

"Wyatt?" I called out.

He turned to face me at the sound of his name, replacing his hat and squinting his eyes at me, trying to place me.

"Wyatt Earp," I said, repeating his entire name. "It is you, by golly."

"Clint Adams," he said, finally finding my name in his memory. He stuck his hand out, saying, "How are you?" and I took it and shook it hard, saying that I was fine.

Wyatt was a young man, twenty-three or-four, tall and slim, very handsome. He was also deadly quick with a gun, and I could testify to that first hand. I'd been facing six gunmen when he stood up from his table and bought into my fight. The arrival of Wild Bill filled out our hand, and we played it and came out on top.

"What have you been up to?" I asked.

"Buffalo hunting. Came to town to pick up my poke from the bank. Sent it here regular, so's it would all be in one place when the hunt was over."

"Smart move. Why don't you let me buy you a drink?"

He looked around. "I'm supposed to be meeting a friend here, but perhaps he's inside. I'll let you buy me a drink if you'll let me stand the second round."

"You've got a deal," I said, and we walked into the saloon together.

"See your friend?" I asked.

"Not yet."

"Well, he'll be one drink behind when he arrives," I told him.

"Or two," he offered, and told the bartender what he wanted.

When the bartender brought our drinks, we clinked glasses and toasted Bill Hickok. Although Bill had fallen on some hard times, I did not bring that fact up when Wyatt proposed the toast.

"What are your plans now that the hunt is over?" I asked him.

"I'm supposed to meet my friend here. We're going to pool our money and open a gambling house and saloon."

"Where?"

"We haven't decided yet."

"You might be better off in Texas, Wyatt. I think Kansas has had its fill of gambling and gamblers for a while."

"Which way you headed?" he asked.

"Just out of Kansas. I've been in this state way too long. One of my horses threw a shoe or I wouldn't be here now."

"Maybe we can travel a ways together," he offered.

"Sounds good to me, but I don't know when my horse will be ready. Man had to finish a job he was doing before he worked on my animal."

"Well, my friend isn't here yet. Maybe by the time he gets here you'll be ready to leave."

"Could work out just right," I agreed.

He finished his drink. "I got to get over to the bank and get my money."

"How much you talking about?" I asked.

"Don't rightly know. Guess I'll find out when I take it out," he said.

"I'll wait here in case your friend shows up.

What's his name?"

"Bartholomew Masterson," he answered.

"Barth—" I started to repeat, with a grin.

"Yeah, I know, he don't rightly like it much either. His friends just call him Bat," he explained. "Bat Masterson."

Chapter Three

Wyatt left to go over to the bank and I ordered a beer.

He told me his friend wasn't quite as tall as him, and was just about nineteen years old, though wise beyond his years. Hell, this Bat Masterson was just about twenty years younger than I was. Seemed to me that there was also something vaguely familiar about the name, although I couldn't place it just then.

When the bartender brought me my beer I wondered if maybe Wyatt's friend wasn't registered at the hotel already, and figured I'd just go over there and check and see. I drank the beer down, wiped my mouth on my sleeve and left the saloon.

You develop a sixth sense when you been a lawman for as long as I had been, and you learn to go with it some. The two men who were riding into town had a shifty look to them, and for that reason they caught my attention. Neither of the pair was much older than Wyatt, and they were dressed in the manner of buffalo hunters, which was another reason for me noticing them.

I watched from the boardwalk as they rode past

13

me and I could see that they were heading in the direction of the bank. I slipped the leather thong off the hammer of my holstered gun and stepped down off the boardwalk. I figured I'd mosey down to the bank, just in case my old lawman's instinct was on target.

They reined in their mounts a couple of storefronts short of the bank and dismounted. The shorter one leaned over and said something to his taller companion, who nodded. They then split up, the shorter one staying on the near side of the bank, and the taller one crossing to the other side. I thought they were setting the bank up, but when Wyatt walked out and the short one signaled to his friend, I realized what was happening.

I drew my gun and broke into a run, shouting, "Wyatt, watch out!"

My shout turned him in my direction, leaving his back exposed to the taller man. The shorter man was hurriedly drawing his gun, now that the element of surprise was gone. His chance to back-shoot Wyatt had passed, and I knew he didn't have a chance in hell of outdrawing Wyatt Earp.

I concentrated on the taller man behind Wyatt, who was similarly drawing his gun in a great hurry. As fast as he might have thought he was going, however, to my practiced eye he seemed to be moving in slow motion. I even waited until he had fully drawn his gun before I fired once, and then again, both shots punching holes in his chest just inches apart.

As he started to fall I glanced at Wyatt and the other man, but the shorter man was already clutching his chest and falling to the ground.

I holstered my gun and walked up next to Wyatt, who was turning the fallen man over.

"He's dead," he announced.

I didn't have to look at the other one to know that he was dead, also.

"So's the other one," I told him. "You know them?"

"Yes," he said, holstering his gun. "They were on the hunt with me."

"I guess they figured to take your money from you."

"And backshoot me in the process," he added. "And they would have, if it hadn't been for you. Thanks."

"This just makes us even," I reminded him.

He nodded, and at that point people began to approach, including a large, rawboned man wearing a badge.

"What happened here?" he demanded with his gun drawn.

"You can put your gun up, Sheriff," I told him. "All the shooting is over."

"What happened?" he repeated.

"These two yahoos attempted to shoot this man in the back as he came out of the bank," I explained. "As you can see, they didn't succeed."

"Thanks to him," Wyatt added, pointing at me. "He warned me."

"Who shot these men?" the lawman asked.

"I shot that one," I said, pointing to the taller of the two dead men, "and my friend shot this one."

"Did anyone see what happened?" the sheriff asked the crowd that had gathered.

A couple of men raised their hands to indicate

they had, and he told them and us, "I'll need you all to come to my office and make a statement."

"Certainly, Sheriff," I agreed. Wyatt, the two men who claimed to be witnesses, and I all followed the tall, lanky sheriff to his office. The lawman was forty-five or so. He competently recorded the statements of the two witnesses, who told the story—remarkably—just the way it had happened. When he allowed them to leave he turned to us.

"What's your name?" he asked Wyatt. When Wyatt told him he asked how to spell it and wrote it down. He then took Wyatt's statement, and turned to me.

"Your name?"

"Clint Adams," I told him.

"You the one they call 'The Gunsmith'?" he asked.

"I've been called that, yeah," I told him.

"Well, I reckon you know what I want then, you having been a lawman and all."

I knew what he wanted, and gave him the story exactly as it had occurred.

"You gentlemen plan on staying in town long?" he asked.

"Just until a friend of ours arrives," I said.

"Well, I don't see any reason to keep you here and send for a circuit judge. Your story checks out pretty well. Did you know those men?"

"I did," Wyatt said. "I can give you their names, if you like."

The sheriff took out a new sheet of paper and copied down the names of the two dead men. The name Jerry Martin rang a bell, but, as with the name of Wyatt's friend, I just couldn't place it.

That done the sheriff told us we were free to leave, and asked us to avoid any further trouble.

"Trouble is the last thing we want, Sheriff," I assured him. "Believe me."

"All right, Mr. Adams, Mr. Earp. Thanks for your cooperation."

"We've both been lawmen, Sheriff," I said. "We know how much easier the job can be when people cooperate."

"That's the truth," he agreed. We bade him good day and left his office.

"What now?" Wyatt asked.

"You got your money?" I asked.

He nodded and patted his pocket. "Nigh on two thousand dollars."

"That's a goodly sum, all right. I was on my way to the hotel to see if your friend was checked in when I spotted those two bushwhackers stalking you. Why don't we go over there now and check? If he's not there we can get ourselves a room while we're waiting for him."

"You decide to travel with us, then?" he asked.

"A ways, maybe."

"You got any money you might be looking to invest?" he asked.

"I might. As long as I'm out of Kansas when I'm investing it."

"I think that can be arranged," he said, and we started over to the hotel.

Chapter Four

Bat Masterson had not yet registered at the hotel, so Wyatt and I did, taking separate rooms. When Masterson arrived, he could share Wyatt's room.

We went to get Wyatt's horse and walked it to the livery, where we both removed our gear and carried it back to the hotel.

"I could use a bath," I remarked.

"So could I."

The desk clerk directed us to the rear of the hotel, where a bath was available for ten cents. If you wanted a hair cut and a shave to go along, it would come to thirty-five cents. A bath and a shave was two bits, and that's what we both took.

Spruced up and smelling of lilac water we decided to check the town out for action—meaning cards, or women, or both.

"That saloon we were in was too small a place for any real action," I pointed out. "There must be a bigger place."

Once again it was the desk clerk who gave us directions to the best saloon in town, and I tipped him four bits for the information. Once outside, Wyatt insisted on giving me two bits, to split the tip.

"If we're going to be partners, we're going to have to start splitting expenses down the middle," he reasoned.

"I haven't said anything about becoming partners, yet," I told him.

"You will."

"Your friend Masterson might have something to say about that," I said.

"Bat won't mind."

"How well do you know each other?" I asked as we made our way to the saloon. Wyatt cut a handsome figure, all spruced up and wearing a gun on each hip. My clothes were somewhat shabbier than his, and my gun was worn from much use. He wore a flat-brimmed black hat. Mine was lighter and slightly chewed up. Wyatt tipped his to two young ladies, who tittered and stole shy glances at him.

"Not so much better than you and I know each other," he finally answered. "We met before I took to buffalo hunting, and we got on real well. We agreed to go our separate ways and meet here to see how much money we each made."

"You worried about him not being here?" I asked.

"Bat can take care of himself."

"So can you," I told him, "but you weren't beyond needing some help a while before, were you?"

"You've got a point," he said, rubbing his lean jaw.

Inside the saloon we heard music and commotion. When we entered through the batwing doors we saw it was nearly three times the size of the place we had been in before. It was not as large as the largest saloons in Abilene, but it was impressive for a town the size of Caldwell.

"Nice," Wyatt commented, "but nothing near what we're going to have."

"You've got big plans."

"Those are the only kind to have."

At the bar we each ordered a beer. The two mugs filled to the brim with brew, not half filled with brew and topped off with foam.

It was getting on towards evening and the place was in full swing. The girls were circulating, doing their best to get the cowboys to spend their money.

"What's your pleasure?" I asked Wyatt. "Drink, gambling, or girls?"

"Well, I'm kind of partial to all three," he told me, "but if I had my druthers, I'd probably pick girls."

"Ah, to be young again," I said, raising my mug. He laughed and raised his as well.

One of the girls sauntered over to Wyatt. She was a cute little thing with dark hair and a green sequined dress. Her adolescent face was heavily made up. Her breasts were pushed up, probably by a corset, and they were creamy and smooth.

"Can I interest you in some fun, Mister?" she asked Wyatt.

"How old are you?" he asked her.

"Not much younger than you, I reckon. What about your friend here?" she asked, turning to me and bumping me with her little breasts. She was looking at me, but still talking to him. "I'll bet he'd like himself a nice young girl to spend some time with." Then she looked up at me challengingly and added, "Wouldn't you, Mister?"

"Not if I have to pay for her I wouldn't, little lady."

She looked hurt and pushed her lower lip out at me like the child she very nearly was.

"I'd be worth it, Mister," she promised.

"I'm sure you would, sweetheart. Maybe my young friend here would be interested. What do you say, Wyatt?" I asked him, grinning.

"Ah, I like my women a little older," he told me. "Why don't you take her upstairs and give her a try?" he asked.

"Robbing the cradle is not a habit of mine," I told him.

Now she pushed her lower lip out again and stamped her little foot.

"If one of you *gentlemen* don't come upstairs with me, I'm going to lose my job."

I looked at Wyatt and said, "We can't have that, Wyatt. Go ahead up with her, I'll keep an eye out for Bat."

"I'll tell you what, Clint. Let's flip a coin."

"Who gets to go with her, the winner or the loser?"

"The winner can either go or stay. It's his choice," Wyatt proposed.

"I'll tell you what," she decided. "Why don't you two big spenders just screw yourselves?"

And with that she flounced away to find someone who wasn't quite as picky.

"Guess we both missed out on that one," Wyatt observed.

"Looks like."

"What about that one?" he asked, inclining his head to indicate another girl across the room.

This one was about twenty-five, and didn't need a corset to emphasize her breasts. They were full and round and just naturally overflowed her red dress. Her hair was auburn and her smile ready and full of promise.

"I wasn't kidding about not paying for it," I said, "but you go ahead. Maybe she likes younger men."

"I'll let you know, Pop," he threw back, and started across the room towards her. It took him all of five minutes to get her to take him upstairs. I sighed heavily at the enthusiasm of youth and ordered another beer.

Chapter Five

I woke up next morning with a rich thatch of auburn hair on the pillow next to me. Trying to clear the cobwebs from my head I attempted to remember where I was and how I had come to be there. The girl next to me stretched her arms over her head, causing the sheet to fall away from full, firm breasts, and moved a warm leg on top of me.

"Good morning," she greeted when she realized that I was also awake.

"Good morning."

"You're a little confused, right?" she asked.

"A little," I told her. "It comes with age."

"Oh, you're not so old. I can testify to that. You screwed me sore, last night."

"I did?"

"You mean you don't remember?"

I shook my head and said, "Sorry, but I don't."

"Well, maybe we can jog your memory," she told me.

She pressed those round, smooth breasts against my face. I automatically reached for a nipple with my teeth and tongue.

"Oh, yeah," she breathed as I sucked and bit it until it hardened into a little stone.

Her hand snaked down between my legs and began to stroke me until I was long and hard, I

23

rolled her over and continued to work on her breasts, then worked my mouth down over her rib cage, over the soft swell of her belly, through the tangle of pubic hair until I found the little nub I was looking for, which was eager for attention.

"Oh, my God," she moaned as I gave it all the attention it could possibly want. I felt her belly tremble. She lifted us both off the bed as she climaxed. I crawled back up until we were chewing on each other's tongues and when she parted her legs I thrust myself deep inside her so hard that she let out a little scream into my mouth.

Her hips began to move and I caught her tempo and matched it, content to let her go as fast or slow as she wanted. Her fingernails dug hard into my buttocks as she pulled me in deeper yet. I reached around and cupped her buttocks with my hands, driving deep.

"Does this . . . bring it all . . . back . . . to you?" she asked in between thrusts.

"I think . . . we should . . . keep it up . . . a little longer . . . until I'm sure . . . I have it."

She seemed perfectly agreeable to that. Before I could explode, she pushed me out and turned over on all fours. I parted her buttocks and drove myself into her from behind, reaching around to cup her breasts.

"Oh, that's it," she moaned, over and over, "that's it, that's it!"

Well, I kept that up as long as I could, but after a while she turned over again and we resumed the missionary position. In a matter of moments, she shouted out once and for all, "That's . . . it!"

And it was.

Chapter Six

"How'd you like my present?" Wyatt asked me at breakfast.

"I liked it fine, but it wasn't really necessary," I told him.

"You wouldn't say that if you had seen yourself last night. You looked so lonesome, I just had to do something to cheer you up."

"What would really cheer me up is getting out of Kansas."

"You must have had a bad experience," he said.

"I've had a bad run of luck," I explained, telling him about almost losing Duke, my big black stallion.

"Losing that gorgeous animal would have been a heartbreak," he observed. "You lucked out there."

"Bad luck he took sick, but good luck he got well. That kind of cancels each other out."

"And you think getting out of Kansas will change your luck?"

"It can't hurt." I poured out the last drop of coffee and said, "After this I'm going to check and see if my horse is shoed."

"Bat should be here today. We can get a move

on by tonight. You make any decisions about becoming partners?"

I drained my coffee and stood up. "Why don't we see how much cash Bat comes up with, and then you can tell me how much you need? I'll let you know if I think it's worth it then, okay?"

"Fair enough."

"I'm going to check my team."

"See you later."

I went over to the livery and found my horse shoed and ready to go.

"Do you want me to hitch them up, sir?" the livery man asked.

I thought about it a moment, then figured, What the hell, I could give Masterson the rest of the day.

"No, not yet. I'll be leaving either tonight, or tomorrow morning. I'll let you know when."

"Okay by me."

"Take care of the big boy, huh?"

"Be my pleasure. He sure is a beauty."

"Yeah, well, he's been sick and could use some more weight. How about some extra feed?"

"No problem."

"Much obliged."

I gave him some more money and went looking for Wyatt. I found him at the Caldwell saloon.

"A little early for a drink, isn't it?"

"It's early to start," he admitted. "I just consider that I'm still drinking from last night."

"Listen, where's Masterson supposed to be coming in from?" I asked him.

He shrugged. "Can't say as I rightly know. Could be anywhere." He looked at me and asked, "You staying?"

"I'll give him another day, Wyatt, then I'll be moving on."

"Suit yourself. Drink?" he asked me, as the bartender came over.

"Yeah, I guess I'll have a beer."

When the bartender brought it over, I asked Wyatt, "What was that girl's name last night?"

"She was something, huh?"

"She was damned good. What was her name?"

"Lynda."

"You going to try her again tonight?" I was really only making conversation, but if he had no intention of being with her again, I was considering breaking my rule of never paying for a woman.

"Well, I thought I'd try that little one, you know?"

"The baby?"

"Well, she wasn't all *that* young. Besides, Lynda says she's worth it."

"Yeah," I laughed, "she told us so herself."

"Maybe one of us should see if they're both right."

"Be my guest."

At that point the sheriff—whose name was Bates, by the way—walked in and said, "Ah, there you are. I've been looking for you two."

"Problems, Sheriff?" I asked.

"Not for me, but for you, maybe."

"Why's that?" Wyatt asked.

"Well, this guy that you killed," he said, talking directly to Wyatt. "The one whose name was Jerry Martin?"

"What about him?"

"Seems his old man's name is John Martin."

"Bull Martin?" I asked.

"That's him."

"Who is Bull Martin?" Wyatt asked.

"He's got the biggest spread in Oklahoma," I told him.

"He's also got a large spread right outside of town," the sheriff said.

"Here, in Kansas?" I asked in surprise. Not only did Martin have the largest spread in Oklahoma, but some people said he *was* Oklahoma. A lot of people always wondered why he was content to stay in that state; it appeared he'd finally decided to branch out.

Just our luck.

"And he's brought his sons with him," the sheriff added, "and some of his, uh, hands."

"Great," Wyatt said, in disgust.

"And you killed one of his sons yesterday," the sheriff told Wyatt. "The youngest one."

"That's even better," I said.

"You guys planning on staying in town much longer?" Bates asked.

I couldn't really blame him for that.

"Don't worry, Sheriff. We'll be on our way as soon as our friend gets here," Wyatt told him.

"Today, I hope," Bates said.

"So do we," I assured him. "We're just as anxious to avoid trouble as you are."

"Glad to hear it. I'm going out there now to let Mr. Martin know what happened."

"Sheriff," I called out as he started away. "You will tell him exactly what happened, won't you?"

He narrowed his eyes at me and said, "I'll do my job, Mr. Adams. Don't you worry about that."

"Oh, I'm not worried," I told him, "not worried at all, Sheriff. Thank you."

When he left Wyatt asked me, "You know this Bull Martin?"

"I know of him," I answered. "As far back as I can remember, even when I was a young lawman in Stratton, Oklahoma, Martin was a power in that state."

"And he's never branched out before now?" he asked.

"He always seemed content with being *the* man in Oklahoma," I told him. "And his sons were always his pride and joy."

"How many does he have?"

I thought a moment, "Four now."

"Are they all thieves?"

"No, not from what I've heard. One is a lawyer. I think I heard that he has political ambitions. The others just run the ranch."

"So I guess I killed the black sheep, eh?"

"I guess so, but I don't think that'll make a difference to Bull Martin. Black sheep or no, he was still one of Bull's sons. His youngest, at that."

Wyatt looked at me appraisingly for a moment, then asked, "Do you want to pull out?"

"Pull out? How can I do that? I thought we were partners?"

He smiled and replied, "So we are," and told the bartender to bring two more drinks.

Chapter Seven

Was I taking on a piece of a fight that wasn't mine? I didn't think so. After all, it could have just as easily been my bullet that killed Jerry Martin.

No, if there was a fight—and I felt sure that Bull Martin would see that there was—then a portion of it was rightfully mine, and I always accepted what was rightfully mine.

However, there was no reason for us to go looking for the fight, or even to stay there and wait for it. If Bat Masterson showed up before Bull Martin sent his telegram, all well and good. We'd be on our way, and if the fight caught up with us, fine. If, however, Bat didn't show up by the time Martin got word of his youngest son's death, we'd be right there waiting when he rode into town, with as many of his sons as he could gather up.

Knowing something of Bull Martin, I felt sure the most we'd have to face would be him and his four remaining sons. He'd keep the fight confined to his family, which would at least let us know what we were facing: five men, five guns. Assuming Wyatt's friend Bat handled a gun well, I guessed we could hold our own.

Wyatt and I scared up a couple of cowboys look-ing for a poker game, and played low-stakes poker for most of the day, just to kill the time. Once in a while Wyatt would get up and walk over to the doors and glance outside, then shake his head at me and return to the table.

As the day wore on, the faces of the other players changed and the stakes went up a bit. When the stakes got a little too high Wyatt sat out, figuring since we were partners there was no point in our bumping heads. We had been splitting the pots anyway up to that point, so he cashed in and went to the bar.

As he stood up to leave, though, I asked him, "You worried yet?"

"Worried? No, but concerned," he told me. "I'm going to grab a drink, and then check the hotel again."

"Okay, partner. I'll see you back here."

"Right."

While he was gone I took just about every other pot, simply because I was that much better than anyone else at the table. They were all cowhands who had finished a hard day's work and came to town to relax and blow off some steam. None of them had the necessary concentration of a good, competent poker player.

Naturally, there was one sore loser. Born losers never blame themselves for losing.

"Mister," one big cowhand finally said, "I think there's something funny going on here."

"The funniest thing I've seen," I told him, "is the way you've been playing cards."

That drew a laugh from the other men at the

table, but a cold stare from him changed that. Apparently all of the other men knew him, and were afraid of his size. He must have been six-four, with wide shoulders and massive hands. Judging from his face he'd been in plenty of fights before, but his knuckles looked as if he doled out more punishment than he took.

"I'm talking about the way you're playing, friend," he said from between his feet.

"You want to be more specific?"

"I don't think all of the cards you been dealing have been coming off the top of the deck," he said.

I leaned on the table and looked him right in the eye.

"If my memory serves me correctly, friend, that hand I just won was dealt by you."

Again, a few men at the table snickered, and that caused him to redden. He jumped up, knocking his chair over, and the whole room went quiet.

"I think I'm going to take you apart, Mister," he told me.

My right hand was out of sight under the table, and I told him, "That might be a little hard to do, friend, with a chunk of hot lead in your belly."

His eyes narrowed as he tried to decide whether I was bluffing or not. I didn't want to give him too much time to think about it.

"Well come on, friend. Everybody's waiting. Make a move one way or the other, towards me or out the door."

His big hands flexed open and shut a couple of times, and he licked his lips as his eyes held mine. When his eyes flicked away for a moment, I knew I had him. Once his eyes moved from mine, he couldn't bring them back to meet mine again, and he was lost. Abruptly, he turned on his heels and stormed out the door.

"Somebody's going to pay for what you just did, Mister," another man sitting at the table told me.

I brought my right hand back up and set it on the table—empty.

"Only if they want to," I told him. "That kind of man will back away from any kind of pressure."

"Jack's just plain mean," the same man said. He was holding the cards in his hand, as the deal had just passed to him.

"He didn't look so mean to me," I told him. "You going to sit on those cards, or deal them?" I asked.

"I'm going to deal them," he assured me, and proceeded to do so.

I won that hand, too.

Chapter Eight

When Wyatt returned it was clear he sensed something had happened. I shook my head to indicate that it was nothing serious. He went to the bar for a drink, and in a few moments I noticed him talking to the young girl from the night before. She was pressing her slim body up against his, apparently having forgiven him for the night before. When I caught a third ace for a full house, I paid attention to my cards. When the hand was over and I looked up, both he and the girl were gone. It didn't take a whole lot of brains to figure out where they were off to.

Somebody was standing at my elbow. When I looked up I saw that it was Lynda.

"Hi, there," she said. "Remember me?"

"Of course I remember you, Lynda."

She looked surprised and said, "Well, I'm flattered. Can I get you a beer?"

"Please," I answered, and she went off and came back with a full mug.

"You going to do this all night?" she asked me.

"Until something better comes along."

She leaned over and said into my ear, "Let me

circulate a bit and earn my keep, and then we'll see if we can't do something about that."

She gave me a good look down the front of her dress before straightening up and going off to mingle with the crowd. I watched the gentle sway of her hips as she walked away from the table.

"Your deal, Mister," somebody said to me, and I turned, took the cards and dealt them out.

At that moment a man came running into the saloon, yelling, "Hey, Big Jack is picking a fight with some poor dude who just rode into town!"

"See," the cowhand who had spoken about Jack before said, "I told you somebody was going to pay, Mister."

"Is that so?" I said. couldn't sit there while the big man took his anger at me out on some poor dude, so I threw my cards in and said, "Let's see about that."

I joined the crowd of cowhands who were filing out of the saloon to watch the fight. I followed them down the street to the livery and saw the big man facing a smaller man right in front of the stable.

"What happened here?" I asked somebody.

"Jack was going in while the dude was coming out and they walked into each other. Big Jack was already mad about something, and he's trying to get him to fight."

"C'mon, you little dude," Jack was shouting. "I'll teach you to look where you're walking."

"I would prefer not to fight you," the other man told him, and I got the impression that he was telling the truth. He wasn't afraid to fight the big man, he would just have preferred not to. "However," he added, "if you insist."

The dude was wearing a black suit jacket and a string tie, and as he spoke he began to remove the jacket. When he was half in it and half out of it, the big man stepped in and swung at him without warning. The dude did a neat little sidestep, stuck out one foot and Big Jack went sprawling in the dirt.

He took his jacket off and asked, "Would someone hold this, please?"

"I got it," I said, stepping forward and taking it.

"Thank you," he said.

"Hat, too?" I asked.

He glanced up as if he'd forgotten he was wearing one, and then took it off and handed it to me. It was rounded on top, instead of flat, and I think they called it a "bowler."

He turned back to the big man just as he came up off the ground with a roar. Again, he sidestepped Jack's attack, but instead of tripping him up this time, he swung a neat right hand, catching the larger man on the cheek as he went by. Once again, his opponent found himself face down in the dirt.

"Shit!" Jack shouted, spitting dirt from his mouth. There was a welt on his cheek where the smaller man's punch had caught him.

"I'm gonna break you in half!" he yelled as he struggled to his feet.

This time the smaller man stood his ground, swinging another right hand that stopped the big man dead in his tracks. He switched his attack to the belly, hitting Jack once, twice and then again, folding the big man almost in half, and then he threw a tremendous right which straightened the big man momentarily, until gravity took over and Big Jack just keeled over backward and lay motionless in the dirt, soundly beaten and out cold.

The dude proceeded to brush the sleeves of his white shirt, then walked over to me and took his coat and hat back.

"Much obliged," he told me, slipping the coat back on.

"It was the least I could do, since I'm the guy that got him mad enough to pick a fight with the first man he saw, which just happened to be you."

"I believe that turned out to be his misfortune, didn't it?" he asked, putting his hat back on and patting it into place.

"Yeah, it sure looks like it," I agreed.

The sheriff came rushing up, bellowing, "What's going on here?"

"Just a small disagreement," I told him. "Both parties settled the matter between themselves, Sheriff."

"Big Jack?" the sheriff asked. He looked at me and said, "You did that?"

"Not me, Sheriff. This gentleman here had that pleasure," I said to him, indicating the slim youngster standing next to me.

"You?" the sheriff asked incredulously, gaping at the young dude. "You took Big Jack in a fair fight?"

"At his insistence, Sheriff. I did not wish to fight."

"That's right, Sheriff," I told him. "It was a fair fight."

The sheriff walked over to Jack and bent over,

peering at the man's face. When he straightened up he said to us, "I ain't never seen Big Jack unconscious before."

"Well then, I'm glad I was able to oblige the law," my new friend said.

"What's your name, friend?" the sheriff asked. "I'd like to tell Jack when he comes around just who it was planted him this way."

"Then you may tell him that he had the pleasure of being knocked out by Bartholomew Masterson."

"Masterson?" I asked, in surprise.

The youngster turned to me and said, "Yes, but my friends call me Bat."

Chapter Nine

When I properly introduced myself to Bat Masterson, he told me that he'd heard about me from Wyatt and was glad to finally meet me. I took him over to the saloon to buy him a drink and wait for Wyatt.

"Where is he?" Bat asked.

"He took some little girl upstairs for some friendly conversation," I told him.

"That figures."

I ordered two beers from the bartender, who looked Bat up and down and asked, "Is he old enough?"

Someone who had seen the fight between Bat and Big Jack leaned in and told the barkeep, "Even if he ain't, he deserves it for what he just did to Big Jack Foster."

The bartender accepted that and set two beers up in front of us.

"Wyatt was expecting you yesterday," I told Bat.

"I got held up by a long poker game."

"How'd you do?"

"I doubled my money, which I figure makes it

worth the wait. Anything exciting happen while you were waiting?"

"Funny you should ask," I told him and explained about Jerry Martin and his friend.

Then I explained about Bull Martin and his other four sons.

"You expecting Martin to come a-running when he hears?" he asked.

"I'd say it's a safe bet."

"Then maybe we'd better finish our beers and get a move on. There's no point in inviting trouble, and staying here to wait for it would be the same as inviting it."

"I agree with the first part, but leaving now wouldn't make sense. It'll be dark soon, and if Bull Martin makes a move against us in the dark, our chances wouldn't be so good. I suggest we spend the night and hightail it in the morning."

Bat winced and said, "I dislike the word 'hightail,' Clint."

"Poor choice of words, sorry."

"But I agree that we should wait until morning. What about our friend upstairs?"

"I figure our friend ought to be just about finished—unless that little girl screwed him to death."

"That's a possibility."

As if to prove that it wasn't, Wyatt chose that moment to appear at the head of the stairs and start down, with the girl in tow.

"Jesus, you weren't kidding when you said she was a little girl, were you?" Bat asked.

The girl heard him and bristled.

"You ain't all that much older than me yourself, sonny," she snapped at him with her hands on her hips. "You want to try your luck upstairs?" she challenged him.

Bat just sneered and turned his back on her, drinking his beer. Wyatt whispered something to her and she giggled and walked away. He then walked over to Bat and clapped a hand on his friend's shoulder.

"About time you showed up," he told him.

"You didn't seem to miss me much," Bat replied.

Wyatt called for a beer and the three of us drank up. Bat and I explained our reasoning to Wyatt and he agreed that we should wait until morning before leaving.

"And if we're going to do that," Wyatt added, "there'd be no harm in you giving Celeste a try, Bat."

"Celeste?" he asked, looking interested.

"That 'little' girl I just came downstairs with."

"That child?" Bat snorted.

"Clint?" Wyatt asked, turning to me.

I held up my hands and said, "If she's a child to Bat, imagine what she must appear to be to me. I prefer Lynda, myself."

Shaking his head, Wyatt said, "You guys will never know what you're missing."

"Who's Lynda?" Bat asked, once again looking interested.

Chapter Ten

Bat didn't have a chance to find out about Lynda or Celeste, not that night. Wyatt paired off with Celeste, and I went with Lynda. The girls brought a friend in for Bat, and he wasn't too disappointed. She was a blonde, about nineteen, with large, round breasts and a pair of the saddest eyes you'd ever want to see. The next morning, Bat looked like he'd had less sleep than either Wyatt or·me.

"That blonde—" he said at breakfast, shaking his head.

"What was her name again?" I asked.

"Lacey Jane," he told me.

"Is that a first name or first and last?" I asked. He shrugged.

"I don't know. She said, 'Call me Lacey Jane,' so that's what I did. Whew, that girl has got energy!"

I finished my breakfast first and stood up.

"Where are you going?" Wyatt asked.

"To check on Duke and my rig. I'll meet you at the livery when you've finished and we can get moving. I can't wait to get out of Kansas."

"Yeah, we know," Bat said. "We've heard it often enough."

"Yeah, well once we're out of Kansas, you won't

hear it anymore," I told him. "That's a promise."

"One we'll hold you to," Wyatt promised back.

When I stepped outside onto the boardwalk in front of the hotel I got a bad feeling. I took the leather thong off the hammer of my gun and stepped down into the street. I'd learned over the years to trust my feelings, my instincts, without question.

This time was no different.

As I started to cross the street three figures stepped off the boardwalk across the street and fanned out, with about ten feet between them.

The one in the middle was Big Jack Foster.

"Well," he drawled, "I wondered who would be the first to come out. I think I would of liked it better if the little one had been first, but I'll take you."

"C'mon, Jack, stop talking and let's get it done. We got to get back. If Bull knows we came in when we was supposed to be sealing the town—"

Now I knew that my bad feelings had to do with a lot more than just these three cowboys spoiling for a gunfight.

Bull Martin had sealed off the town and Big Jack had sneaked in with two pals to settle his score.

"You want to settle your score, Jack?" I asked him.

"Yeah, friend, I wanna settle my score. No, I wanna settle more than my score. I wanna settle you—right into the ground."

I shook my head and looked at each of his two friends in turn.

"Jack's lucky you guys came along," I told them.

They exchanged nervous glances with each other before one of them finally decided to be the one to ask, "Why's that?"

Looking Big Jack right in the eye I said, "Now he won't have to die alone."

It was very early in the morning still, and if anyone was watching what was going on he was well hidden. But for the four of us, the street was empty.

If things went wrong, soon there would only be one of us. If things went right, there'd be three. If Big Jack backed off, there'd be four of us left alive, but the only thing I was sure of was that I would come out alive. I knew my own abilities, and I could gun down the three of them before any of them cleared leather.

But I didn't want to. I would avoid killing any of them, if I could—and I hoped I could.

But it was not to be.

Pride does a lot of things to men, some good, some bad, but the worse thing it does is get them killed.

That's what it did to Big Jack.

It was the only thing that made him go for his gun. I saw his eyes flicker and his hand move. I even had time to check the other two men and see that they were out of it before I finally drew my gun and shot Big Jack through the heart. All three of us watched him slump to the ground, gun still in his holster.

"You men made a wise choice," I told them, holstering my own weapon. "Now go back to your boss and tell him to make one, too."

"I've never seen anything like that," one of them said.

"Go back and tell your boss what you saw. Tell him his son took his own life, he just used someone else's hands to do it. Tell him I could have killed all three of you, but I didn't."

With a last glance at Big Jack's body they started to walk and then ended up running for their horses. As they drove away Sheriff Bates came up behind me.

"I heard what you said, Adams," he told me. A crowd was beginning to form now, and even Wyatt and Bat came out to see what the commotion was. "It won't make a difference, though," Bates added. "Not to Bull Martin."

"What's going on?" Bat asked, coming up alongside of me.

"Friend of yours came to call," I told him. "Sorry I couldn't wait for you."

He bent down to see who it was, then grunted and stood up.

"Who is it?" Wyatt asked.

"The guy I played with yesterday," Bat told him. "I guess he came back for more and got too much."

"Some of you men want to move him?" Bates called out to the crowd.

"Should we get going?" Wyatt asked.

"Yeah, to the saloon," I told him. "Sheriff, I think you should come along, too. This involves your town. You may be in the middle of a war."

Chapter Eleven

"You mean Martin's got this whole town sealed off?" Bat was incredulous.

I shrugged. "I haven't checked it out, yet. Maybe he's only got all the roads closed off. If we stay off them we may be able to get through."

"And if we wait?" Wyatt asked.

"Hold on," Bates spoke up. "I don't want a shootin' war in my town."

"Then I suggest you ride out and talk to Bull Martin, Sheriff," I told him. "We won't make a move until you talk to the man."

"I'll do it," Bates said, standing up. "I ain't afraid of Bull Martin."

"Yes, you are. But you'll talk to him anyway, because you're a good lawman."

He may have felt insulted by the first half of my statement, but the last part appeased him just a bit.

"I'll let you know what happens."

When he was gone Wyatt leaned in close and asked me, "What do you think is going to happen, Clint?"

"I don't know, Wyatt. I guess it depends on just how much of what I've heard about Bull Martin is true."

"You think one or both of those other two cowboys that came in with Jack were his sons?" Bat asked.

"It didn't seem that way to me," I replied. "I don't think a son of Bull Martin's would follow around a dumb shit like Jack Foster."

"So we just sit and wait?" Bat asked.

"For a while, anyway."

We ordered three more drinks, and when we had them Bat asked me, "Why didn't you just gun the three of them, Clint?"

"Because I didn't have to," I said. "I was able to talk them out of backing Jack's play, and by doing so I sent a message back to their boss."

"I think gunning the three of them might have been a more effective message," Bat reasoned, and it was the reason of youth talking. I didn't argue with him, I just hoped that my own reasoning would bear out, and that he'd learn from the results.

"There's another thing we ought to consider," I told them.

"What's that?" Wyatt asked.

"Martin may want to come into town himself, at the very least to claim his boy's body. While he's here he may want to size us up, see how many of us are involved. He knows about Wyatt and me, but he may not know about you, Bat."

"Hold on. I ain't leaving—" Bat started to argue, but I cut him off.

"I wasn't suggesting that, Bat, but you could stay in the background, just in case Martin does show up. There's no use in tipping our hand. We have an ace in the hole, we might as well keep it there."

"I guess that makes sense," Wyatt agreed.

"Okay, I'm for that," Bat agreed, reaching into his jacket pocket. "But speaking of aces in the hole," he told us, coming out with a deck of cards. "Who's for a little poker?"

I sat forward, unwrapped my hand from my beer mug and said, "Why not?"

Chapter Twelve

"Sheriff's riding back in," the bartender said some time later, "and he's got company." He turned and looked at the three of us from his place by the window.

"Bring three more beers, Nathan," I instructed him.

"Who do you suppose the company is?" Wyatt asked.

"I don't suppose," I said, standing up. I walked and looked out from over the batwing doors.

I'd never seen Bull Martin, but it wasn't hard to pick him out. The other three men were riding well behind him, even the sheriff. Only two were his sons, but he commanded the same respect from the three of them.

Wyatt came up next to me and handed me my fresh beer. Bat came up on my other side.

"That's Bull Martin, is it?" he asked.

"I guess," I replied.

The three of us watched the four men ride to the undertaker's. To our surprise, the sheriff and the other two men dwarfed the man called "Bull" Martin. Oh, he was built like a bull, all right, but he stood barely five and a half feet tall. The way he stood and the way he moved, commanded respect. There were plenty of bigger and stronger men, but over the years he'd proved there weren't many smarter, or more ruthless.

I hoped he was intelligent enough to listen to the sheriff's story and to realize his son's death was his own fault.

Bull Martin entered the undertaker's office first, and the other three followed.

"The sheriff looks like Bull Martin's tail," Wyatt observed.

"Let's not judge him too harshly until we hear what the story is," I suggested.

"Spoken like a true lawman," Bat laughed. Wyatt nudged him, indicating that he too had once worn a badge. "Okay, gang up on me," Bat told us, and we all laughed.

"I think maybe I should go across and give my condolences to Mr. Martin on the death of his son," I decided.

"Isn't that pushing things?" Wyatt asked.

"No," I told him, "if you went, it would be pushing things," referring to the fact that it was his bullet that actually killed Jerry Martin. "Why don't you two guys keep playing two-handed," I suggested. "Maybe with me gone one of you can finally win a hand."

As I approached the door of the undertaker's, Bull Martin came walking out. He stopped short when he saw me. The sheriff sidled out from behind him, while the other two men were pinned inside, behind their boss, or father.

"Sheriff," I greeted him. "Mr. Martin, I presume?"

"Who are you?" Bull Martin asked me, then he turned to the sheriff and repeated the question. "Who is he?"

"Mr. Martin, this is Clint Adams," the sheriff told him.

"Adams?" Martin asked, looking back at me quickly. He had no neck that I could see, and thick shoulders and arms. He'd have made a hell of a more impressive figure if he hadn't had such short legs. His eyebrows reflected what was probably the color of his hair, gray. He looked to be in his late fifties or early sixties.

"Are you the man who killed my son?"

"I was there, yes," I replied.

"No, no," he said. "I want to know if you're the man who put the bullet into him."

I was about to say yes, but the sheriff jumped in and said, "It wasn't Adams, Mr. Martin. He killed the other one."

"I'm sorry about your son, Mr. Martin," I told him, "but he brought it on himself."

"I'm going to show you what kind of man I am, Adams," Martin told me. "I'm going to let you ride out of town, because you didn't kill my son."

"It could just as well have been me, Martin," I told him.

"But it wasn't," he said. "It was your friend, and he's the one I want. You're free to go."

I shook my head.

"It doesn't work that way, Martin. We're a matched set. If you're going to go against him, you've got to go against me. It really isn't necessary, though. Your son—"

"My son was my son, and that's all I care about," he told me. "Wes, Jim?" he called, and the other two men stepped around him onto the boardwalk.

"He was their brother," Bull went on, "and that's all they care about. Now I'm going to give you one more chance, Adams. Ride out of town."

I looked at all of them for a long moment and then shook my head. "Not a chance, but I'll give you the same advice. Ride out of town and forget it. Your boy wasn't worth the loss of more lives."

"Why you—" the one called Wes started, and I watched as his hand made for his gun. His old man saw it too and he moved faster than I would have thought possible. He grabbed his son's arm with both of his hands and for a moment I thought he was going to break it.

"Don't!" he shouted, holding tight.

"But Pa—"

"He'd kill you before you could touch your gun!" Martin roared at his son. "Jim," the old man said over his shoulder.

"Yes, Pa?"

"Drop your gunbelt."

Jim Martin, who was almost as big as Big Jack Foster was, dropped his gunbelt to the walk. He wasn't as tall as Foster had been, but he had his father's shoulders and arms, thick and well-muscled.

"Now," Martin said, taking his hands off his son Wes's arm, "you drop yours."

Wes undid his gunbelt and let it drop.

"Mr. Martin—" Sheriff Bates started.

"Quiet, Sheriff. There's not going to be any gunplay here," the old man said. "Not unless Adams here wants to gun down two unarmed men."

"And if he doesn't, they'll stomp him to death," the sheriff added. "I can't let that happen, Mr. Martin. Not right here in front of me."

"Then turn around," Martin told him, "or go to your office, or to the saloon, or to the whorehouse." Looking at me the old man told him, "This is going to be a fair fight."

"Fair?" Bates asked. "Two against one?"

"Hey, this here's the man they called the Gunsmith," Martin said. "He's used to these odds, aren't you, Mr. Gunsmith?"

I stared at them, all of them, and then undid my buckle and let my gunbelt fall to the ground. I hoped Wyatt and Bat would be smart enough to stay out of it.

"See, Sheriff?" Martin said. "Don't kill him, boys," he told his sons. "I don't want the Sheriff to feel that he'll have to arrest you when you're finished."

"Yes, Pa."

"Right, Pa."

Both "boys" stepped down into the street, confident smirks on their faces. Jim was bigger and stronger and more dangerous. Wes, he thought he was unbeatable because his brother was there with him. Jim just thought he was unbeatable.

Right off they made a mistake, and I took advantage of it. They came at me too close together. I threw a lefthanded backhand across Wes's left cheek, and followed with a right hand to Jim's left cheek.

Wes was knocked clean off his feet, Jim just staggered back a step, obviously better able to take a punch than his brother. He immediately launched a right at me that I ducked under. If it had connected it would have taken my head off. I stepped inside his extended right arm and began to pound his belly and ribs. When he started to bring his arms around for a bear hug, I stepped to the side, and then behind him and threw a vicious punch to his left kidney. As big and strong as he was, that dropped him to one knee.

I turned to find Wes back on his feet, but he was staring at his brother in disbelief. I didn't give him a chance to regain his composure. I hit him with a right and grabbed his shirt with my left hand so he wouldn't fall before I wanted him to. Holding him that way I hit him three more times, then let him go and watched him slump to the street. When I turned Jim was just starting to get his breath back. Before he could rise I wanted to send my boot into the side of his head, but before I could something hit me in the back, just above my own left kidney. It was off the mark, but hard enough to knock some of the breath out of me.

Bull Martin hadn't been able to stand by and watch his sons take a beating, so he'd stepped down into the street to join the fray.

I dropped down to one knee, pretending I was hurt more than I was. Thinking I was now easy prey for his son Wes, Bull Martin backed up and stood next to the sheriff again.

Feeling brave again, if not angry, Wes Martin advanced on me again. He threw a right that I misjudged. I thought I'd be able to avoid it, but I only avoided part of it. The part that I caught felt like the kick of a mule and I went down on my back in the street. I knew what was coming and started to roll away, but part of his kick caught me as well, sending waves of pain through my side. As he approached me again I hooked one of his ankles between my feet and twisted, bringing him down too. I got back to my feet first and was waiting for him when he climbed to his. I hit him with two quick rights, but all they did was cut his lip.

"Damn," I said, because my hand ached from hitting him in the face. He rushed me and caught me up in a bear hug. Before he could get completely set to crush the air out of me, I clamped my hands over his ears and thumbed his eyes for good measure. He dropped me, not knowing where to grab first, his ears or eyes. I took one step back and kicked him between his legs, which solved his problem of what to grab. He sank to the ground, his mouth open and his hands on his crotch.

I turned and found Bull Martin going for his six-gun, but a voice called out, "I wouldn't do that, Martin."

It was Wyatt, alone, and his gun was leveled at Bull Martin's belly. Bat had been smart enough to keep our ace in the whole and stay out of it.

"Who the hell are you?" Bull asked him.

"I'm the man you're looking for, Martin," Wyatt told him. "I killed your son, and what's more, he deserved killing."

Martin's spine stiffened and if looks could kill Wyatt would have been dead on the spot.

I went over and picked up my gunbelt, strapped it back on. That done, Wyatt put up his gun, inviting Martin to go for his.

"Any time you feel lucky, Martin," he told the old man.

Bull Martin actually considered it, I could see that in his eyes, but he finally turned to the Sheriff and said, "I want this man arrested for assaulting my sons, Sheriff."

I watched the sheriff to see how he would react. He didn't like it and it showed in the disgusted look on his face, but he told Martin, "Like you said, Mr. Martin. It was a fair fight. No reason to arrest anybody."

"You're with them, then," Martin accused.

"I'm with my town, Mr. Martin, and I don't want it shot up. This is all unnecessary. These men are right, your son caused his own death. These men didn't go looking to kill him."

"Ah," Martin replied. He stepped down into the street and began kicking his two "boys" until they struggled to their feet.

"Get on your horses, you no good—" He walked over to his own horse and mounted up. He pointed at the sheriff and said to him, "You're with them, as far as I'm concerned. I got enough men out there to burn this town to the ground, and that's what I'll do unless you send these two men out to me. You think about it, and you tell your townspeople to think about it." To me and Wyatt the old man said, "I'll be seeing you boys again."

"I wouldn't look forward to it," Wyatt told him.

His sons struggled up onto their horses and with a last look of hatred for the three of us, Bull Martin led them out of town.

"I'm not looking forward to it either," I said, half aloud. "Not one bit."

Chapter Thirteen

When the Martins were out of sight Bat came out of the saloon.

"That wasn't half bad," he told me. "If the old man hadn't stepped in you would have cleaned those two boys without a mark on you."

"Yeah," I replied, feeling my cheek where he'd hit me, and then rubbing my ribs, where he'd kicked me.

"It wasn't very diplomatic, though," he was quick to point out. "In fact, it might even have made things worse."

"I'll have to go along with that," the sheriff said, stepping over to us. "You boys have put me on the spot."

"Why?" Bat asked. He obviously hadn't heard what Bull Martin had said about burning the whole town down if the sheriff didn't hand us over, so we repeated it for him.

"I see. That really does put you on the spot, doesn't it, Sheriff," Bat agreed.

"It surely does," the sheriff said bitterly, and then turned and stalked away.

"What do you think he'll decide to do?" Wyatt asked.

"I don't know," I said, "but we'll try and make a move of our own before he makes a decision."

"A move of our own? Like what?" Wyatt asked.

"How the hell do I know?" I asked. "It was my idea to come over here and talk to Bull Martin and look how that one worked out. You two guys come up with something. I'm going back to the saloon to rest my old bones."

"We'll walk with you, old timer," Wyatt said, "so's you don't fall down on the way."

So I limped on back to the saloon with Wyatt and Bat on either side of me and took a chair in the corner while they went up and got three beers.

As they sat down with me Lynda appeared at the top of the stairs and when she spotted me she came rushing down.

"Clint, are you all right?" she asked.

"Sure, little girl, I'm fine," I told her.

"I saw what happened from the window," she told me. "I think you were wonderful—no thanks to your two friends!" she added. They exchanged amused glances and continued to watch her fawn over me.

"Are you sure you're all right?" she asked, touching my face where Jim Martin had hit me.

"Just a little sore in the ribs," I told her, touching my side to show her where.

"I saw that big brute kick you when you were down," she said. "Why don't you come upstairs and soak in a hot tub?" she suggested. "That'll keep it from stiffening up."

Actually, once I thought about it, that wasn't such a bad idea, especially considering who was offering me the bath.

"That sounds good, Lynda." I got to my feet. "You two bright boys can let me know what you've come up with when I come back down."

Wyatt leaned over and said to Bat, "If he comes back down, he means."

I went upstairs with Lynda. She walked beside me all the way, in case I fell—as if she could have caught me. She took me to a room in the back of the second floor with a large, metal bathtub, and while I undressed she filled it with hot water.

"Get in," she said. "I'll be right back."

I slid inch by inch into the steaming hot water until it was working away at the ache in my side. The little girl had a good idea here, and I leaned back to enjoy it.

"Scrub your back?" I heard Lynda's voice ask. When I opened my eyes to reply I was frozen by the sight of her.

She'd pinned up her long auburn hair, and only a few loose strands still hung down, one on her forehead, one alongside her neck. The green ribbon she used to tie it up was all she wore. Her breasts were full and round, with large brown nipples and a sprinkling of freckles in the valley between. She was long waisted, odd for a girl barely five foot three.

"I said—"

"I heard what you said," I assured her. "Go ahead, scrub away."

She grabbed a wash cloth and approached the tub.

She began with my back, using first one hand, then the other.

"Move forward," she said suddenly. She got into

the tub, put a leg on either side of me, and continued scrubbing.

"Now your chest." She moved up closer and I could feel her wet breasts pressing as she reached around and began to wash my chest. She rubbed it with a circular motion, and at the end of every circle she got lower and lower. Soon she was rubbing my belly, and the cloth was forgotten, having sunk to the bottom of the tub. With her left hand she grabbed a handful of my pubic hair, and with her right she grabbed a handful of me. Slowly, tantalizingly, she began to stroke the full length of my wet penis until the blood was pumping through it like crazy. She reached with her other hand and began to execute a two-handed pumping action that had me ready to blow.

"Get around in front," I commanded.

"All right, but I don't want to get out of the tub to do it," she told me. She stood up, lifted one foot over my shoulder, and then swung the other over my head.

"Wait," I told her. She leaned back, with her hands on the rim of the tub. I reached underneath her, cupped her buttocks and lifted her up. She put her legs up on my shoulders and I moved closer so I could hold her up and reach her with my mouth.

I began to execute some circular motion of my own, circling her clit with my tongue. She started to squirm in my hands, but I held her fast and continued tonguing her. Soon she began to make small whimpering sounds, churning her hips, grinding herself against my face.

"Oh, God, oh Clint," she moaned. Her thighs closed tighter around my head, as if to keep me from pulling away. I had no intention of stopping until she came. I could feel the tremble building up in her belly, and her little nub got very hard before she finally achieved orgasm, half whispered, half screamed.

I lowered her bottom until she was back in the water, with her legs on either side of me again. She leaned her head against the side of the tub, looking at me with a dreamy expression on her lovely face.

"Mmm, I was the one who was supposed to relax you," she told me.

"I'm relaxed."

She looked down at the head of my swollen penis, as it broke the top of the water from time to time and said, "I don't think that's really true."

She reached out with both of her hands and began to fondle me, tickling my scrotum, stroking me until I couldn't take it any longer.

"Come here," I told her. I reached for her and put my hands on her waist, drawing her to me. I slid my hands down and cupped her buttocks again, only this time I lifted her just enough so I could slide in. We were together and she began to ride me up and down, sloshing water over the side of the tub and onto the floor.

"Oh sweet Jesus," she moaned. "I've never done it under water, before."

Even after I shot inside of her, she rode me, keeping me hard until she experienced another orgasm.

With me still inside of her she reached forward and kissed me, thrusting her tongue deep into my mouth. I ran my hands over the wet skin of her back, slid my finger along the crack in her ass. The whole situation was keeping me aroused, and I wanted her again, but in a bed, this time.

"Let's go to your room," I told her. "I want you in bed, underneath me."

"Oh, yes," she breathed against my mouth, kissing me again.

We dried off and I started to pull my pants on.

"Don't bother," she told me. "All the other girls are in their rooms. Come on."

Feeling ridiculous, but excited, I followed her down the hall, watching her bare buttocks undulate as she trotted ahead of me.

Once inside her room we wasted no time.

"Deep, Clint," she told me, lying on her back and spreading her legs for me. "I want it deep."

I obliged her, although I could only go as deep as I was long, but that seemed deep enough for her.

She wrapped her legs around my waist and we quickly found the tempo that fit both of our needs. Slow and easy, enjoying the tantalizing build up towards release.

"Oh yes, darling, yes," she said in my ear. "I love it, I love feeling you in me."

She must have said those words many times before, with fat cowboys sweating over her, old ones laboring over her, but whether she meant them or not this time didn't matter to me. After that fight out in the street I needed this, and that was all I cared about.

She began to whimper in my ear, louder and louder. Finally, at exactly the same time, we both came. It might have been a testament to her judgment and timing, but I felt that her orgasm was real, and not playacting.

If she was acting, though, she was in the wrong business.

Chapter Fourteen

"How are your ribs feeling?" Wyatt asked when I went back downstairs.

"Fine," I answered, signaling to Nathan the bartender to bring me a beer. "The hot bath helped a lot."

Bat leaned forward at that point and started studying my face and hands, looking for something.

"What are you looking for?" I asked, accepting a full beer mug from Nathan.

"Wrinkles," he answered. "If you were in the bathtub all this time, you should be wrinkled up like an old lady."

Wyatt leaned forward, as if on signal, and said, "I don't see any wrinkles, do you Bat?"

"Nope, not a one," Bat said. "I guess he must have gotten out of the tub sometime."

They wore the same smirk on their young faces.

"All right, you guys, funtime is over. Time to stop picking on the old man. Did either one of you bright boys come up with a decent idea about what we should do?"

They exchanged different kinds of glances then, and Wyatt was the one who spoke.

"The way we figure, we have no way of knowing what we're up against unless we take a ride and see just how badly we're bottled up here. Once we know that, we should be able to figure a way out of town and be on our way."

"With Bull Martin on our trail," I said.

"For how long?" Bat asked.

"How old was his boy?"

"Look, Clint, maybe he'd come after us, and maybe not, but who'd go with him? His other sons, sure, but how many of his men would be willing to go running all over the country? We don't know how many men he's got with him now, but how many would still be with him when he caught up to us?" Wyatt asked.

"You would rather run than fight?" I asked, wanting to see what their reaction would be to the word "run."

"I don't know about you or Wyatt," Bat said, "but if he's got twenty, maybe thirty men out there with him, I'd feel like a fool going up against him now."

"I agree with that," Wyatt said.

"So do I. I'm glad to see that you two don't exhibit the impatience or stubbornness of most men your age."

"Like you did when you were our age?" Wyatt asked.

"Not me," I answered. "I was always as level-headed as I am now."

"Tell me about it. I remember Wild Bill telling me stories—"

"Let's worry about the present, not the past, okay?"

"Have it your way," he said.

"Okay, I will. The only question now is who rides out to scout the situation. I vote for me."

"Why you?" Bat asked.

"I've got the best horse," I told him.

Bat looked at me a moment, then said, "Not that big black in the stable."

"That's the one," I said.

"Well, I can't argue that point," Bat agreed.

"Neither can I, but why don't two of us go?" Wyatt asked.

"Why not the three of us?" I offered. "Same reasoning. One of us will be harder to spot, it's that simple."

"After dark?" Wyatt asked.

"I'll have less chance of being spotted that way," I agreed.

"You better watch you don't break your neck riding around out there in the dark," Bat advised.

"That's a detail I'll leave to Duke," I told him.

"Duke?"

"His horse," Wyatt explained.

"As surefooted as a mountain cat," I said, proudly, and I was very proud of Duke, who I had raised from a yearling. As large as he was—and I'd never come across another horse nearly as large in the five years I'd had him—he was remarkably surefooted.

"He must be a very special animal," Bat said.

"He's unique," I answered.

Wyatt called out to Nathan for three more beers.

"Poker while we wait for dark?" Bat asked, producing a deck of cards.

"I'm all for that," I said.

"Good," he said, dealing the cards out for five card stud. "Maybe when you're out of money I could persuade you to put up that horse of yours for one hand of showdown."

"That's not likely," I told him. "I'd just as soon put up my right arm . . . or my gun."

"That shows you how highly he regards that horse, Bat," Wyatt told him. "Why don't you show Bat that gun of yours, Clint. I've told him about it, but I'm sure he'd like to see it himself."

I don't usually take my gun from my holster unless it's to use it, or to clean it, but I make an exception from time to time, and I made one now. I produced my gun and put it on the table. Bat picked it up and began to examine it.

"Interesting," he remarked.

"It is a basic Colt design, with two major differences," I told him.

"A solid body," he observed.

"And double-action, not single."

"Increased speed, I can see," he said. "But doesn't that cut down on your accuracy?"

"For accuracy you can still cock and fire, rather than pull the trigger alone, but the double-action has come in handy many times, I can tell you that."

He hefted it, sighted with it, then reversed it in his hand and returned it to me. I holstered it and looked down at my cards. He had dealt me four hearts up, and one in the hole. The hole card was an ace, which gave me an ace high flush.

I was about to make my bet when the batwing doors swung inward and a girl stepped into the saloon. All activity stopped, including ours, and all eyes took in the new arrival.

She wasn't very tall, and she was a little chunky for my taste. Her shoulders and breasts were especially broad and full, making her small waist seem even smaller by comparison. Around that small waist was strapped a holstered sixgun.

Her hair was long and dark, and her face was very pretty and somewhat familiar, yet I was sure we had never met before.

"I'm looking for Clint Adams," she announced to the room at large.

I looked at my companions, who were also looking at the girl, then raised my hand and said, "You've found him."

She turned her head at the sound of my voice, located me and approached the table.

"I would like to speak to you, Mr. Adams."

"Go ahead."

"In private."

"Would it be all right if I knew who wanted to talk to me?"

"My name is Jerri Martin, Adams," she told me, staring down her pretty nose.

"Martin?" I asked.

"That's right. Bull Martin is my father."

Chapter Fifteen

I stared at this girl, who appeared to be all of nineteen, and realized why she had seemed familiar to me. She resembled her father. Neither of her two brothers, Jim and Wes, had resembled their old man, but she did, and in spite of it, she was attractive.

"I see. Well, what is it I can do for you, Miss Martin?" I asked. I couldn't ever remember hearing that Bull Martin had anything but sons, but if the girl was telling the truth, she was obvious truth to the contrary.

"Like I said. I want to talk to you alone," she repeated.

"Where would you suggest this talk take place?" I asked.

She looked around the room for a moment, then took a deep breath and looked back at me.

"Your hotel room."

I looked at Wyatt and Bat, who were amused, and said, "Gentlemen, it looks like this game will have to go on without me—at least, temporarily."

I stood up and held out my hand towards the door.

"Miss Martin?"

She hesitated only a moment, obviously not used to being treated like a lady, then went on ahead of me.

As we walked to the hotel she admitted, "With nothing but brothers around, I'm not used to being treated like anything but another brother."

"Well, you don't look like anyone's brother to me," I told her. She might have smiled, but I couldn't see her face clearly, so I couldn't be sure. No other words were spoken until we got to my room. On the way up, the clerk threw me a knowing look that I ignored. If Jerri Martin had seen it, she might have thrown a couple of shots his way, so he lucked out there.

I watched her behind ascend the steps ahead of me and thought that it really didn't look half bad. Tight, round and firm—just a little chunky, otherwise it would have been perfect. From the way she wore that gun, I figured she knew how to use it.

When we got into my room I offered her a drink from a bottle in my saddlebag, which she refused.

"Then I guess we can get right to it then. What was it you wanted to talk to me about?"

She walked up to me and put her hand on my left arm. Her eyes were violet, and very beautiful. They were staring right into mine.

"One thing I wanted to do was see the man who beat up my brothers, Jim and Wes, and who made my Pa back down. That would take a lot of man," she told me.

Her eyes swept over me from head to toe a couple of times, making me feel like a side of beef.

"Well?" I asked her. "Do I pass?"

"Oh, yes," she replied. "You look like a lot of man, all right."

She ran her tongue over a full underlip, then bit that juicy looking lip. Her eyes, her mouth, her entire face was sensuous, but her body could only be described as . . . solid. Large breasts and hips, sloping shoulders. There was no question in my mind but that she was who she said she was, Bull Martin's daughter.

She was desirable, but not in the way that Lynda was. Lynda was beautiful, fragile, and you wanted to hold her, cuddle her, make love to her. Jerri Martin was more of a challenge. Desirable without being sexy. You just *had* to know how this girl was in bed.

Maybe later, I'd be able to find out. Right now, though, I wanted to find out what she wanted with me.

"Now that we've established that, would you mind telling me what you want with me?"

She dropped her hand from my arm and backed away a little, hooked her thumbs into her gunbelt.

"I want you to leave town, Mr. Adams," she told me. "I don't want my father and my brothers to kill you and your friends. I also don't want you to kill any of them. One brother is enough."

"Wait a minute, Miss Martin—" I started, but she stopped me short.

"I know, you're going to tell me that my brother Jerry was no good and was asking to be killed. I believe you, because I knew Jerry. We were very close, Jerry and I, and it was more than just having the same name. We were so close that I knew what he was, so I wasn't surprised when he got killed.

My Pa's different, though. I'm the youngest, but Jerry was always 'the baby,' if you get my meaning."

"I believe I do."

"Then you realize that it doesn't matter to Pa why Jerry was killed. All that matters is getting the man who killed him."

"And you don't want that?" I asked, frowning. "As much as you say you loved your brother?"

"You're not listening to me very well. I didn't say I loved my brother, I said I knew him. Better than anyone else in the family knew him. We were the closest in age, we played together as kids. The others were always older. But to answer your question, no I don't want the man who killed him to die. I don't want anyone else to die, Mr. Adams." She walked up to me again and put her hands on my chest. "I especially don't want you to die."

"Me? Why not?"

"Because," she said, reaching up to put her hands around my neck and pulling me down with surprising strength, "you interest me, very, very much."

She pulled my face down near her and kissed me, gently at first, and then brutally, savagely, like a thirsty man having his first drink of water after coming off the desert. I really had no choice but to respond. She thrust her tongue into my mouth and I bit it, hard. I tasted blood, her blood, but that only seemed to excite her more.

"Oh, God," she breathed, taking her mouth from mine, drawing a long, shuddering breath. "I want it," she told me, "I want it bad."

I would have thought that I was all tuckered out

from my session with Lynda, in the tub and out, but to my surprise, I wanted it bad, too. I wanted *her,* to satisfy that question in my mind.

She backed away and began to unbutton her blouse. When she removed it I was pleasantly shocked. Her skin was smooth and milky, but that wasn't the surprise. Her breasts, which had appeared chunky while she was dressed, were actually the most beautiful I had ever seen. They were almost perfectly round and incredibly firm. The nipples were large and an odd color, which only added to their attraction. They seemed to be almost gray, if it wasn't the light in the room.

"Surprised, huh?" she asked, obviously pleased by my reaction. "Thought I was just a fat little—"

I reached out and grasped her breasts hard, causing her to gasp, and said, "I never thought that." I tweaked her nipples to life with my thumbs and she grasped my wrists in her strong hand.

She threw her head back as I continued to play with her nipples. She had practically no neck, but her neck was not my concern. Those incredible breasts were.

Her hands left my wrists and traveled down to my pants. First she undid my gun and let it drop to the floor, then she undid my pants.

"Let's get it done right," I told her. I released her breasts and started to undress. She did the same, dropping her gun to the floor and removing her boots and pants.

When she was naked she stood before me, waiting to be inspected. Her waist was trim, her hips full. Her thighs and legs were well-muscled, maybe a shade too heavy for her height. All in all her body demanded to be used, and I intended to use it.

I drew her to me and lowered her to the bed. I began to nibble her breasts with my mouth, squeezing them together at one point so I could suck on both of them at once, which seemed to drive her crazy.

"Oh God, Adams, I want it bad," she breathed. She reached down then and encircled my penis with one of her hands, and gave a low, throaty laugh. "You want it too, don't you? You can't wait to try me out."

As an answer I raised my body above her and then lowered all of my weight onto her. As I had thought, she was able to take it. I licked her full lips, then kissed her deeply, nibbling on the lower one. At the same time I pinned her hands above her head. She thrust her powerful hips against mine, rotating them. I sank my penis into her and she cried out, "Oh God, yes, that's it. Do it, please!"

I began to stroke, in and out, and her cries increased in tempo and volume until finally she screamed as she came, and then screamed again when she felt me filling her.

"Yes, yes. . ." she kept saying again and again.

I released her pinioned hands and prepared to dismount, but she wouldn't allow that. She threw her arms around me and grabbed my buttocks, holding me prisoner within her.

"Not yet, I want more," she told me. She started doing something with her vagina that was making me get hard again. It felt like a wet hand, yanking on me until I was bone hard again, then she began to move her hips in a circular motion. I sought her tempo, found it, matched it, and we were off on another ride.

"You're something, aren't you?" I asked her, and she wrapped her legs around my waist and replied, "Oh yes, yes, yes."

I reached down underneath her and took hold of those chunky buttocks. I could feel them clenching and unclenching powerfully, as if they had a life of their own.

"That's it, it's happening," she said suddenly, increasing her tempo. "Oh yes, God, that's it," and then she screamed again and I filled her again, just as strongly as before.

"Mmmm," she moaned, running her hands over my buttocks before unwinding her legs from around me. "You are a special man."

"And you're a puzzling little lady," I told her, sliding off of her and lying beside her. "What's this all about, Jerri?" I asked. "Did your father send you?"

"Jesus, no. If he knew I was here—" she said, shaking her head.

"Then why did you come?"

"All of my reasons were true," she told me. "It's just that there was another one, and we just finished it."

"Just like that, you wanted to go to bed with a man you never met?"

"The man who whipped Jim, and backed my Pa down, yes," she replied. "You know, if my brothers knew about this, they'd have a whole different reason for wanting to kill you."

"Is that so? Like to protect their little sister, do they?"

She laughed.

"That's not it at all. They like to pass me around," she told me, and then added, "don't look so shocked. After a while I didn't even mind anymore. I just pretend like it's not happening until they're all finished."

I hesitated to ask, and then asked anyway.

"Even your father?"

She laughed again, without humor, but without bitterness, too. An odd, empty kind of laugh.

"Especially my father. He was the first one, when I was fourteen."

"And it's been going on ever since?"

"When things get slow, or when they can't find any whores. Actually, it doesn't happen as much as it used to." She rolled over and put her hand on my chest, adding, "And it was never like it just was with you. You're the first, you know—the first who wasn't my brother, or my father. I always wondered if I'd be able to respond to a man."

"And?"

She put her head on my chest now and said, "Couldn't you tell?"

"Yes," I said, putting my arms around her, "I could."

"Don't feel sorry for me, Clint," she told me. "I guess I could have run away any time, but where would I go? They're my family."

I guess that made sense to her, but it didn't to me. I didn't argue, though. It probably wouldn't have done any good.

"Now more than ever I want you to leave town. I don't want anyone getting killed."

"Well, then, we want the same things, Jerri," I assured her. "There are just a few things we have to know before we can leave."

She picked up her head and looked at me.

"What are they?"

"How many men your father has with him."

"He's got my four brothers, and about fifteen or twenty others," she told me.

"How well have they sealed off the town?"

"They have both roads covered, but beyond that I'm not sure."

"Then I'll still have to ride out there and take a look. We've got to know just how well we're boxed in before we can figure out a way out."

"You know, I was afraid you'd be the kind of man who wouldn't want to run, who would stay and fight, even if it meant getting killed."

"You're describing a fool, Jerri, and neither my friends nor I are fools. We'll fight when the time comes, but this isn't the right time or place."

"How can I help?"

"You already have, just don't let your father know about it," I advised her.

"Don't worry, I won't."

"Jerri, once we get out, how far will your father follow us?"

"Until he catches you," she answered. "That's the way he is."

"What if his hands don't want to go on that long?"

"He'll keep at it, him and my brothers. Eventually I guess you will have to face him," she finished, half to herself, as if she'd just realized that it was inevitable.

"Somebody will have to get killed, then," I told her.

She buried her nose into my chest and shook her head, then looked back up at me.

"I guess I just want to put it off as long as possible," she said.

"I can't blame you for that," I replied. I was hoping that she had been totally honest with me, because I liked her.

Her hand strayed down and began playing with my limp penis, bringing it to life again. She was surprised that I could be ready again so soon. Thinking about Lynda again, I thought that she really didn't know the half of it.

"My brothers, they go once and they're finished for hours. My Pa, sometimes he can't even do it once. But you—"

"You make it easy, Jerri," I replied. "You make it easy, and you make a man want you."

She grasped my rigid penis and began stroking it lovingly.

"Mmm, you talk nice," she said.

She climbed atop me and touched her vagina to the tip of my penis. She let the head penetrate, lubricating her, and when she was very wet she released me and moved down so that she could minister to me with her tongue, her teeth, her lips, tasting herself on me at the same time.

"Umm," she said, filling her mouth with me, and I reached down to hold the back of her head.

I was starting to wish we had all night.

Chapter Sixteen

Jerri Martin had been right. I checked the roads north and south of town and saw they were totally blocked off. Bull Martin had left four or five men at each road. By Jerri's count, that still left roughly about fifteen men to box the town in. That was too little men to cover so much space. There was a way out, all I had to do was find it.

Once I'd established that the main roads out of town were blocked I began to concentrate on points east and west of town. Martin had arranged the remainder of his men into floating patrols which Duke and I were able to avoid without much trouble. It might be harder, though, for three men riding together to avoid them.

There were a few small foot trails through the surrounding brush but they would be impassable on horseback. It was mainly by accident, while avoiding another of Martin's two men, floating patrols, that I found what looked like the way out. Ducking them, Duke and I ducked right into a road that was hidden behind a brush wall. Apparently, the road had been so well used at one time that the brush had grown around it and hidden it, yet it was still wide enough to accommodate not only a few men on horseback, but possibly a wagon. My wagon would have fit, if I had plans to take it, which I didn't. I was going to leave it behind for now and come back for it later. Sneaking out of town precluded taking my rig with me. Much as I hated thinking of it as sneaking out, that's what we were doing, but we were doing it because it was necessary. The townspeople didn't need a shooting war, and we didn't need to stand up to twenty five men and get killed just to prove we weren't afraid.

Trying to leave most of the brush intact, I eased Duke through and started to follow the road. If it went far enough east we could eventually hook up with the main road and then continue on out of Kansas to wherever it was we decided to go.

I was almost ready to turn back when I came upon an old farmhouse. Probably when this farm was active, the forgotten road had been often used. When the farm died the road fell into disuse and was overgrown with brush. Lucky for us, because it looked like our way out.

I checked out the farmhouse itself, found it to be in disrepair but well-built and sturdy. I peered out the rear window and saw that there was another road, not as well used, leading away from the farm. Unlike the road leading in, it was not large enough for a wagon, but it could bear three men traveling single file. I could have followed the road out to see where it led, but wherever that was, it was better than where we were, so I said the hell with it and headed Duke out of there.

Chapter Seventeen

"They call her what?" Wyatt asked.

"That's right," I told him, helping myself to a healthy swig of a much needed beer, "they call her 'Little Bull' Martin."

They both thought that over for a moment, then Bat said, "Well, it seems appropriate. She does look small."

"Maybe the parts you saw," I told him.

Wyatt leaned closer and asked, "Was she really any good?"

"A gentleman never tells," I replied.

"How would you know?" he shot back.

"What did she want, Clint?" Bat asked.

I explained to both of them most of what she wanted and let their imagination supply the rest.

"You think she's for real?" Wyatt asked.

"I think so. She's got a real weird relationship with her family, but they're still her family. I never could understand those kinds of relationships," I said.

"No family?" Wyatt asked.

"No."

"I've got five brothers and a sister, so I can understand it," he said.

"I've got four brothers and two sisters," Bat said.

"I've always wondered what it was like to be part of a big family," I said, "or any family, for that matter."

"It can be very hungry," Bat replied, and we let the subject of families drop.

"What did your little scouting trip come up with, Clint?" Wyatt asked.

"A way out, I think." I described what I had found out, and what I had found.

"Did you time the patrols?" Bat asked.

"I tried, but they don't seem to follow any kind of a set pattern."

"Well, we're not dealing with a military force," Wyatt pointed out, "so that would be a little too much to ask for."

"We can get through, but it will have to be one at a time. We could leave town fifteen minutes apart, and meet at that farmhouse. From there we can go on together."

"When do you want to go?" Wyatt asked.

"As soon as possible," Bat answered.

"We'll need supplies, but we don't know if Martin has any men stationed in town. If they see us stocking up, they'll get word to him. We'll have to buy it a little at a time."

"Why not have Lynda and Celeste buy most of it," Wyatt suggested. "That won't arouse anyone's suspicions."

"As long as they don't buy too much at one time," I pointed out. "Okay, that sounds good. Why don't you guys ask them about that?"

"And what will you be doing?"

I stood up.

"I've got a little bull waiting in my room."

When I returned to my hotel room it was late and to my surprise Jerri was not there waiting for me.

I found myself feeling disappointed, for more than one reason.

The sheets were cool, indicating that she had left some time ago, possibly right after I did. Where had she gone? Back to her father, her family? Had she been sent after all?

No, I didn't think so. Nothing had been accomplished that could possibly have justified her being sent to talk to me, or seduce me. Whatever her reasons for leaving were, they were not to report back to her father about me.

I took out the bottle from my saddlebags, took a quick drink, and then turned in. I thought about Wyatt and Bat, probably very comfortable with Lynda, Celeste or one of the other girls. Then I thought about Jerri, the chunky girl with the beautiful breasts, and I fell asleep.

Chapter Eighteen

At breakfast Wyatt informed me that both girls had agreed to buy most of our supplies for us.

"By the way, Lynda was disappointed that you didn't show up last night," he added.

"Actually, last night I went to sleep alone."

"The little bull was gone?"

"Yeah."

"You know how to get in touch with her?" he asked.

"No, but I imagine she'll be in touch with me. At least, I hope she will. I've still got some questions for her."

"I'll bet," Bat said.

"Should we talk to the sheriff?" Wyatt asked.

"I'll do that," I answered. "You get the girls busy getting those supplies. I'll also talk to the livery man about having our horses ready. I think we'd be better off leaving after dark. It'll be easier to avoid the patrols that way."

"Okay, I'll talk to the girl," Wyatt said.

"I'll buy some extra ammunition," Bat added. "That shouldn't arouse any suspicions. If the girls are seen buying bullets, that would."

"I agree. Let's go. I want to be out of Kansas by morning," I said.

We got up and went off on our respective tasks.

I found Sheriff Bates in his office, cleaning his rifle and pistol.

"You expecting some trouble?" I asked him.

"I'm just getting ready for it if it comes," he answered.

"You'd back us?"

"I'd fight for my town," he said, and I knew I had been right about him. He may have feared Bull Martin to some extent, but he was a good lawman, and upholding the law came first in his mind.

"Well, you'll be glad to know that we're leaving town," I informed him.

"Leaving?" he asked, putting down his gun. "When? How do you expect to get past—"

"We'll be leaving tonight."

"In the dark? That's crazy. They'll—"

"We won't be going by way of the main roads, we'll be going—" I began, then changed what I was going to say, "—another way." I made a snap decision not to let him in on all of our plans. "When Bull Martin comes to town tomorrow, he won't find us here."

"And what if he comes today?" he asked.

"Let's hope he doesn't," I said. "He's probably not yet sure how many he'd have to face if he came into town after us. He'll be content to sit outside of town and make us sweat for a while."

"He'll come after you."

"Probably, but then we'll all be away from your town. Isn't that what you want?"

"Uh, yes, but I still don't want anyone to get killed."

"Well, if we can help it, no one will," I said. "I just wanted you to be aware of what was going on."

"I appreciate that, Adams," he said, standing up and holstering his gun.

"I'll say goodbye now," I added, "in case I don't get a chance later." We shook hands and I started out, then remembered something and turned back.

"Oh yeah, I'm leaving my rig behind. Try and make sure it's still there when I come back for it, huh?"

"It'll be there," he promised. "I just hope you do make it back."

"When I do, I'll tell you the whole story."

"Good luck."

"Thanks."

My next stop was the livery stable. On the way I passed the general store. Little Celeste came out carrying an arm full of packages. I just hoped nobody wondered why a whore would be buying so many supplies.

I looked around the streets as I walked, wondering how many men were working for Bull Martin. Nobody seemed to be paying me any particular mind, but you never could tell.

At the livery I approached the man in charge and asked him to have our horse ready to travel as soon as it got dark. I paid him enough to keep his mouth quiet, but added some incentive before leaving.

"If anyone should find out about this beforehand," I told him, "I'd be forced to come back here looking for you."

"Nobody's going to find out, Mister. You can count on me," he answered.

"Good. Can I also count on you to take good care of my rig and team while I'm gone?"

"You bet, Mister, real good care."

Patting him on his beefy shoulder I said, "I knew I could count on you, friend."

"Sure—sure can."

On the way back to the saloon I caught Lynda coming out of the general store and offered to help her with her packages.

"Why, thank you, Clint," she said, handing them to me. Nothing suspicious in a man helping a pretty woman carry her packages.

"I'm sorry you were too busy last night to come by," she said as we walked.

"I'm sorry, too, honey," I said, not offering any explanation.

"Wyatt says you'll be leaving tonight."

I suppose it would have been too much to ask for her to go ahead and buy our supplies without telling her why. I only hoped that she and Celeste didn't entertain any of Martin's men—or his sons —before we left.

"I've already stayed much longer than I'd originally intended."

"Any particular reasons?"

She was fishing for a compliment, and there was no harm in giving her one.

"Oh, I can think of one or two," I said, smiling at her so that she'd know I was talking about her. She didn't smile back, though. She obviously had something else on her mind, and it didn't take a genius to figure out what it was.

"I heard you left the saloon last night with a woman. At least, some people seemed to think she was a woman."

"Uh, yeah, a girl did come in looking for me. Turns out she was the sister of one of the men we killed."

"Bull Martin's daughter?" she asked in surprise.

"Oh, you know about him, huh?"

"Everybody's heard of Bull Martin. I thought all he had was sons."

"So did a lot of other people."

"The way I hear it, even his daughter looks like a son," she said.

"Some people might think so."

"What do you think?"

"I don't think I should be talking about one girl to another girl," I replied. "It isn't wise."

The answer didn't seem to satisfy her, but we'd reached our destination. We entered through the back way and went up the stairs to Celeste's room. Wyatt was waiting there with her.

"Celeste has agreed to hold the stuff here until we're ready," he said.

"Good. We appreciate this, Celeste," I said, and then turned and said, "You too, Lynda. Thank you."

"Would you like to come to my room?" Lynda asked.

"I'm sorry, honey, but I want to talk to Wyatt for a while."

"Maybe later?"

"Sure, if I can."

She nodded, and backed out, closing the door.

"She's got it bad for you, Clint," Celeste told

me. I turned to look at her. She wore no makeup this early, and she looked incredibly young.

"I thought that was a cardinal sin," I said.

"For a whore?" she added. Before I could reply she said, "It is. We never fall for our customers. If we did, I'd have a thing for this tall one, here," she said, touching Wyatt's shoulder as he sat. He put an arm around her waist and swung her into his lap, where she squirmed contentedly.

"I think I'll go find Bat," I said to both of them.

"Good idea," she said.

Chapter Nineteen

Bat was in the saloon when I went down. Even though it was early, he'd managed to find three pigeons for poker and, from the looks of things, he was cleaning up.

I started to walk over to the table when I caught Bat's eye and he shook his head just enough for me to catch it. I didn't know why, but I changed my direction and headed for the bar.

"What's up, Nathan?" I asked the bartender.

He put a beer in front of me and leaned his bony elbows on the bartop.

"Those boys over there," he said, "are Bull Martin's boys."

"His sons?" I asked, not noticing either Jim or Wes. There were still two Martin brothers I hadn't seen yet.

"No, not all of them," Nathan said. "The one with his back to us, facing your friend Bat, is Ben Martin. The other two are just hands."

I sipped my beer and leaned on my own elbow, watching the poker game.

"I wonder what they're doing in town?" I said, half to myself.

"They came in here looking for whisky and women. Bat there is a right persuasive young man. He convinced them that all they really wanted was a good game of poker, and he's been giving it to them good ever since."

"He would."

Nathan went off to clean a wet spot and I stood there watching the game.

Bat kept talking to those boys, and he had my head spinning, so I could just imagine how they felt. He was getting them to say things they'd never remember saying. He had Ben Martin talking more than the other two, who were concentrating very hard on their cards to no avail.

"So, who's this guy you boys have got bottled up in town?" Bat asked.

"A couple of guys," Ben answered. "A couple of smart guys. One of them's a big time gunny, but that don't impress me none. I use a gun pretty good myself."

"Is that so?"

"Don't I, boys?"

The "boys" nodded their heads, agreeing with whatever the boss's son had to say.

"I was sure sorry to hear about your brother getting killed," Bat said.

"Did you know Jerry?"

"No, I didn't know him, but I got brothers of my own. I know how I'd feel if one of mine got killed."

"Well, maybe if it was Wes, or Jim, but Jerry, he wasn't nothing but trouble. He ain't gonna be missed by none of us, 'ceptin' maybe Pa."

"How far is your pa willing to go to get his killers?" Bat asked.

"Far as he has to, I guess."

"How about you, and your brothers?"

I couldn't see Ben Martin's face, but I assumed he was thinking about something, either the question, or his cards.

"I guess we'll go as far as he does. He's the boss."

"What about the hands?"

"The hands will do what they wanna do," Ben said, sounding annoyed. "Hey, are we gonna talk, or play cards?"

"I call," Bat said, throwing some money in.

Ben Martin began to laugh and spread out his cards.

"Queen high straight," he whooped.

"Ace high straight," Bat said, laying his cards down and raking in his money.

"Shit!" Ben snapped.

"Well, gentlemen," Bat said, folding his money. "Thank you for the game."

"What?" Ben snapped.

Bat looked at him.

"I said thank you," he repeated, standing up.

"You can't leave," Ben told him. "You got our money."

The other two men nodded vigorously, this time needing no prodding to agree with the boss's son.

"That's part of the game, friend," Bat told him, his tone turning ice cold. "Somebody wins, and somebody loses. This time, you lose."

"Oh, no," Ben Martin said, and I knew what was coming. Martin was going to draw his gun, and Bat was going to kill him. That would reinforce Bull Martin's motives for hunting us down.

We didn't need that.

I stood three quick steps and clamped my hand on Ben Martin's arm just as he was drawing his gun. I wheeled him around and hit him once in the jaw, sending him reeling over the table. His two friends were too stunned to move, and by the time they had recovered, they were looking down the barrel of Bat's gun.

"Pick up your friend and get out," I told them.

"You ain't heard the last of this," Ben threatened, struggling to his feet. "My pa—"

"Your Pa would skin you alive if he knew you were here," I told him, taking my first good look at his face. He was younger than Jim and Wes. He looked barely old than Jerri, so I figured with Jerry Martin dead, he was the youngest son, now.

"I wish you would tell your pa, though," I added. "Tell him I gave him one son back, today. Tell him that for me."

Ben narrowed his eyes, taking a good look at me, and said, "Are you the one—"

"Just get out of here, boy. Go back and tell your daddy what I said—that is, if you dare to tell him that you came into town when you were supposed to be outside it. Go on, get out!"

The two hands hustled the boss out of there, before he could get himself, and them, killed. In fact, even if he only got himself killed, they knew that Bull Martin would kill them for it.

"Well, thanks," Bat said, holstering his gun. "You saved his life."

"Yeah, and put you on the spot. If he tells his old man what happened here, he'll know you're with us. And even if he doesn't tell him, *he* knows you're with us. You're in now, Bat, whether you want to be or not."

"I've been in, Clint," he informed me, "right from the start."

"Okay."

We both sat and Nathan brought over a couple of beers.

"Thanks for not shooting up my place," he told us.

"Our pleasure, Nate," Bat answered for both of us.

"I heard some of it," I told Bat. "You didn't get much out of him, did you?"

"They talked a lot, but not about much. The only thing I verified is that the two man patrols aren't on any set pattern. We'll just have to watch our step."

"We intend to," I replied. "We fully intend to."

Chapter Twenty

I left Bat in the saloon, waiting for Wyatt, while I went back to my hotel room to pack.

"Hi, lover," Jerri Martin greeted when I walked in. She was sitting on my bed, fully clothed.

"Well, you come and go, don't you?" I asked.

"I'm sorry I had to leave last night, but Pa would have wondered where I was."

"We wouldn't want Pa to wonder, would we?" I asked.

I started putting my stuff together, and she asked, "Are you leaving now?"

"Soon."

She sat up straight, interest showing on her face. "How?"

"I've figured out a way out," I told her.

Now she stood up and walked over to me, her thighs touching mine as she watched me pack.

"You don't trust me?" she asked reproachfully.

"Don't be insulted, sweetheart," I told her, touching her neck, "there aren't too many people I do trust."

She leaned her neck back against my touch and said, "I want to come with you, Clint. Take me with you."

It hadn't been an altogether unexpected request, not after last night. She knew now that she could communicate with someone outside her family, so now she wanted to get away, on her own.

"Jerri, listen. I'm not—"

"Don't get me wrong, Clint," she hastened to add. "I don't exactly mean that I want to go away with *you*. I just want to go away, and since you're going too, I'd like to travel with you."

"I don't think that's too wise," I said. "Your father will be on our trail as soon as he realizes that we're gone. Why don't you leave on your own?"

She took my hand and held it, like a little girl who's afraid of the dark.

"I don't think I'm quite that independent yet," she said. "Besides, you might have a better chance with me along."

"You mean as a hostage?"

"Why not. How's Pa going to know I went with you willingly? If the need arises, you can use me that way." She put her hands on my chest and added, "If the need arises, you can use me any way you like."

I kissed her once, gently, and her mouth trembled. Then I held her close and she put her head against my chest.

"Jerri—"

"I know. You don't trust me. You don't want to tell me how you and your friends are getting out of town. That's okay, I can accept that, Clint. What about meeting me somewhere? You don't have to tell me how you're getting out, just let me meet you and you can take me along. That way I can't give you away."

That way she couldn't give Wyatt and Bat away. She could still set a trap for me, but as long as I wasn't endangering Wyatt and Bat, I thought I should take a chance on her.

I put my hands on her shoulders and held her off at arm's length.

"All right, Jerri. I'll take a chance on you, but we'll do it my way."

"How's that?"

"Have you got your horse with you?"

"Yes."

"Is there anything at your father's ranch that you can't leave behind?"

"Uh, I guess not. You mean—"

"I mean, you don't go back there, you just wait here in town with me and you leave when I leave. That's the only way I'll do it."

She studied my face for a moment, then said, "All right."

I dropped my hands from her shoulders and paced the length of the room. Looking out the window I said, "There's one more thing."

"What's that?"

I pointed to her hip and said, "That gun. Do you know how to use it?"

She looked down at the gun on her hip, as if she had forgotten it was there.

"I can use it. Pretty good, too."

"Will you?"

"Will I what?"

"Use it?"

She looked at me with a puzzled expression before what I was really asking her finally dawned on her.

"You mean, will I use it against my father and my brothers?" she asked.

"That's what I mean."

She had to think about it for a moment, with her hands pressed together in front of her pretty face.

"I have to be honest, Clint. No, I couldn't use it against my family. The others, yes, because most of them are just hired gun hands, but not my family."

"All right," I said, walking up to her and taking her by the shoulders again. "All right, as long as you're honest, we'll do it."

"When?"

"Tonight," I replied, holding her against my chest again. "We leave tonight."

Chapter Twenty-one

By the time darkness started to fall, we had our gear all packed. I left Jerri in my room and went to the saloon to meet Bat and Wyatt.

"Are we ready to go?" I asked.

"We are." Bat answered for both of them.

"How about one for the road, men?" Nathan asked, producing a whiskey bottle.

"Why not?" I replied. "It might get cold later on tonight."

Nathan poured three drinks and we clinked glasses and downed them. As we set the empties down on the bar I had a fleeting thought, a suspicion about Nathan. He'd been real nice to us all the time we were there, and a lot of times we sort of forgot he was around and might have talked a little too freely about our plans. Nobody ever notices the bartender. Well, now I noticed him, but maybe it was too late. Then again, all he knew was that we were leaving tonight. He didn't know how we were getting out, so how much harm could he do if he wanted to?

"Thanks, Nate," Bat told him when he refused money for the farewell drinks.

"Good luck to you boys," he told us.

"Thanks, Nathan," I said. "Thanks a lot. Let's get going," I said to Bat and Wyatt. "Who's going first?"

"We drew cards," Wyatt said.

"And I won," Bat added. "I decided to let Wyatt go first."

And I had decided to let them both go ahead of me, because I'd have Jerri with me, doubling my chances of being spotted, and if we were spotted ahead of Wyatt and Bat it might close off their escape. As long as they went first, I was not endangering them with my decision to take Jerri along. I hadn't even told them that she was coming. They were in for a surprise when we both showed up at the farmhouse, but by that time any argument would be useless.

"Okay, don't forget. Give him fifteen minutes," I reminded Bat.

"Where are you going?"

"I've got something else to attend to. I'll leave one half hour after Wyatt and meet you both at the farm—at the place we agreed," I said, changing my mind about saying what I was going to say because Nathan was still listening.

"You want to go up and say goodbye to Lynda?" Wyatt asked.

I looked upstairs, then said, "I don't have time. I wish I did, but I don't. Tell her for me, will you, Bat?"

"Sure."

Outside it was now dark and I told Wyatt, "Good luck."

"You too," he replied. He patted Bat on the

shoulder and then walked out the door.

"What's going on, Clint?" Bat asked. "You're acting kind of funny."

"I'll explain later. Don't worry, nothing will go wrong," I assured him, touching his arm.

He studied my face for a long moment, then shrugged and simply said, "Okay."

For want of something better I repeated, "Okay," and then added, "Good luck, Bat."

"This goes against the grain, you know," he commented as I was walking out the door.

I stopped short and said over my shoulder, "I know," and then, when I was outside, I repeated it for my own benefit.

"I know."

Chapter Twenty-two

"Are we ready?" Jerri asked as I entered my hotel room for the last time.

"Just about."

"How long?"

"About twenty-five minutes or so."

She gave me a sly look and asked, "How shall we spend it?"

"That'll have to wait until some other time." She pouted, but I added, "It deserves more time than we can give it now, don't you think?"

She brightened and said, "Yeah, you're right about that."

I brought out the bottle from my saddlebag and said, "Drink?"

"Why not?"

She took the bottle from me and took a healthy swallow. She knew how to drink, that was for sure. Another result of having so many brothers, I imagined. I took the bottle back and sipped a mouthful myself, then capped it and replaced it in my bags. I looked at her and caught her staring out the window at the darkness.

"Scared?" I asked.

She snapped her head in my direction, a denial ready on her lips, but she bit it back and then nodded.

"I guess I am. Not of what we're doing tonight, though. I'm more afraid of what comes after, when we split up and I go on my own," she confessed.

"You'll be fine," I assured her—or tried to reassure her.

She nodded, then stared out the window again and said, "I guess."

I gave her a few more moments with her thoughts, then stood up and said, "It's time, Jerri. Let's get to the livery."

"Right."

She picked up an extra bedroll that I had taken a chance buying for her, and we left the room.

When we reached the street I was glad to find no sign that either Wyatt or Bat had been caught or seen.

When we reached the stable the door was closed but unlocked. The livery man was not in sight, but had left the door unlocked for us.

Inside, I said, "Let's saddle up."

"Right."

She went to her horse. I found Duke and began to saddle him.

"How ya doing, big boy?" I asked him. He nuzzled my hand. "Yeah, I know. I haven't been paying too much attention to you lately."

"Are you talking to me?" Jerri called out.

"No, to my horse." There was no reply.

"I'm ready to go," she called a few moments later.

"So am I."

"I'm afraid not," a third voice said. We both turned and saw the three men standing in front of the front doors.

"Hello, Miss Martin," one of them said. He was standing in the middle, the same one who had spoken before.

I looked at Jerri with what must have been an accusing glance, because she quickly said, "I don't know how they found us, Clint. I truly don't, I swear."

"Your father's been worried about you, Miss," the man said, and the sarcastic accent he put on the word "Miss" told me that he did not customarily address her that way.

"Stop the crap, Post," she told him, and he flinched at the tone of her voice.

"Don't take that high and mighty tone with me, you little tramp," he snapped at her. "I know what your brothers and your loving father use you for, remember?"

"You pig!"

"Me?" he laughed. "I'm the pig?"

He was a big man, unshaven, unwashed and, to a certain degree, unintelligent. I didn't think he was a foreman, or that he held any position of authority.

"How'd you find us?" I asked.

"Just happened to see you coming in here. We was sneaking into town for a drink. Which one are you?" he asked.

"I'm the one who's going to kill you if you don't get out of the way," I answered. They were so overconfident they hadn't bothered to draw their guns.

"Hear that, boys? He's gonna kill all three of us. You think you can do that, friend?"

"Maybe not, friend," I replied. "But I know one thing. You'll be the first to die, and you'll never know what happens next."

He wet his lips and examined my face. Though he was not a leader, the other two were obviously even less intelligent, because they were looking to him for some sign.

"Which one are you?" he asked again, this time his tone showing more interest than before.

I didn't answer, but Jerri couldn't let it go. "He's Clint Adams, the Gunsmith. He could gun down the three of you before you even cleared leather," she told him, then added, "even if I wasn't here to help him."

I was hoping she wouldn't get brave and go for her gun. Shots would alert the town and, possibly, some of the Martin patrols. I was hoping to talk these men out of forcing a gunfight.

"I'd prefer not to, though," I said to them. "I'd appreciate it if you'd all just drop your gunbelts to the ground. You'll stay alive that way."

I kept my eyes on the man in the middle, the one Jerri had called Post. The other two would follow his lead, such as it was. I kept my eyes on his and, as he started to blink more rapidly and wet his lips more frequently, I knew I had him. If Jerri would just keep still a little longer. . .

"Okay, okay," Post said. He undid his buckle and let his gunbelt drop. That galvanized the other two into action and they did the same.

"A wise choice, guys," I told them. "Now turn around, please."

"You're not gonna, gonna—" Post stammered.

"No, I'm not going to kill you, Post. I'm just going to tie you up so you can't let anyone know that we've left. Someone will be along in the morning to cut you loose. Jerri, see if you can find some rope. If you boys will just kick your guns over here? Thank you."

When we had them all tied I emptied their guns and scattered the bullets, then threw the gunbelts up into the hayloft.

"Mount up, Jerri. Stay close behind me, but don't crowd me. Make sure your pony goes exactly where Duke—my horse—goes. Got it?"

"I've got it."

"Then let's ride."

Chapter Twenty-three

Jerri's mount was a surefooted mustang who handled the terrain very well. She followed my instructions and didn't crowd me at all. She stopped when I held up my hand, and started when I waved that it was okay. We avoided a couple of patrols and made it to the beginning of the trail in one piece.

There was no longer any doubt in my mind about whether or not to trust her. She'd had numerous opportunities to turn me in—in the livery, or by attracting one of the patrols—and she'd passed up the chance every time.

"This is it," I whispered.

"This is what?" she asked.

"The way out. Right through here."

Because I had been there before, I could tell that someone had been by there very recently, Wyatt and Bat I hoped. In spite of that, however, the road was still hidden from sight. So well hidden, in fact, that Jerri didn't see it until we were through the brush and on the road.

"Where does it lead?" she asked.

"To a farmhouse. Let's not talk for a while, okay?"

She nodded, and followed me.

I kept my eyes, ears, and nose open for signs of trouble, but everything was quiet. In a few minutes we reached the farmhouse.

"This is it," I said in a low voice.

We entered the clearing where the house stood. I saw two horses tied to a post. I recognized them as Wyatt's and Bat's animals.

"They made it," I told Jerri, but she remained quiet, an odd kind of silence that set my teeth on edge. There was something on her mind.

I rode up to the house and she followed. We dismounted and she tied up her mustang. I dropped Duke's reins, knowing full well he wasn't going anywhere without me. It was kind of an unspoken agreement between the two of us.

As she walked around her horse and came up alongside of me I asked her, "Are you all right?"

"Fine."

"Is something on your mind?"

She didn't look at me so I couldn't see her face when she said, "I'll tell you inside."

As we approached the door it opened and Wyatt appeared in the doorway.

"I told Bat those footsteps I heard were that big black beast of yours," he said.

"You've got good ears, Wyatt," I said, walking in past him.

As Jerri brushed past him he stared down at the top of her head and shut the door behind her. Bat looked up from the solitaire game he was playing, saw her and said, "Jerri Martin."

"Right," I replied.

"Yeah, right, but what's she doing here?" he asked.

"I can explain—"

"And why is she laughing?" Wyatt asked in a totally puzzled tone.

"I—" I began to say, and then I looked at her and she was indeed laughing, silently, but in seconds the sound came bellowing forth, deep and hearty.

"Jerri, why are you laughing?" I asked her.

She held up her hand, indicating that she needed a moment to catch her breath.

"R-riding up here," she began, "I thought this area had started to look familiar, but when I saw the house. . ." she said, and started laughing again.

The three of us just continued to stare at her while she fought for her breath again.

"Here you are," she continued, "trying to avoid my father, and you're sitting in a farmhouse on his land!" And she started laughing all over again.

We weren't laughing.

Chapter Twenty-four

When Jerri had finally stopped laughing—except for an occasional uncontrollable giggle—we sat down around an old table and Bat broke out a bottle of whisky.

"It is ironic, I suppose," I said, as we passed the bottle around. I had just finished explaining why I had brought Jerri along, and we all realized how ironic it all was.

"Pa's only been here once, though," Jerri pointed out. "This farm is just a small tip of what he bought here. There's really no reason for him to come looking here."

"Just the same, we can't be comfortable staying here until morning. We'll have to leave tonight," I said.

They all indicated that they were ready to follow Duke and myself, leaving it to us to pick our way through the dark.

"Once we get to the main road, we can quicken our pace," I said.

"That'll give us a big head start," Jerri added.

"And it'll take them a while to pick up our trail and find out which way we've gone," Wyatt said.

"That brings up another question," Bat said. "Where are we going?"

We all looked at each other for a long moment, and then Wyatt asked, "What are our options?"

"Our immediate options are north to Nebraska, east to Missouri, south to Oklahoma, and west to Colorado."

"Missouri," Bat said, and me and Wyatt both made unpleasant faces.

"Look, we can't travel in a straight line, because that would make it too easy to find us," I suggested. "Let's go down through Oklahoma, cut through Texas and end up in New Mexico. I'm sure we'll find a town down there that needs a good saloon."

Wyatt and Bat exchanged glances, and then Wyatt said, "Sure, why not?"

At that point we all looked at Jerri.

"Saloon?" she asked.

"The three of us are going to pool our money and start a big saloon and gambling house," Wyatt told her.

"At least, that's the plan," Bat added.

"Well, I'm not exactly the saloon girl type," she remarked, "and I haven't really got any money of my own, so I guess once we get clear of here, I'll just go on on my own."

The three of us exchanged glances then, and it was after silent agreement that I said, "Jerri, you can ride along with us if you like, until you feel you're really ready to cut loose on your own. Of course, you might be safer riding alone."

"From my father, maybe, but not from Indians, or bushwhackers. As long as the offer is open, I'll tag along for a while," she decided.

"Okay, there's one more thing Jerri and I should tell you," I said to Wyatt and Bat, and then went on to explain about the three cowboys in the livery.

"You didn't kill them?"

"Shots would have brought the whole town and Martin's men down on us. And once they'd dropped their weapons, there was no reason to kill them. They should be there until morning."

"Unless somebody notices them missing and goes looking for them," Wyatt said.

"Well then, let's get started now," I replied, taking a last swig from the bottle. I handed it to Jerri, who drank her share and passed it on to Wyatt.

Outside Wyatt asked, "Have you checked this road any further along?"

"No. I figured it didn't matter where it led, it's our only way out."

"As long as it doesn't lead straight to Bull Martin's main ranch," Bat pointed out.

"Don't worry, it won't. Pa's ranchhouse is twenty miles from here, at least."

"Well, I just hope he's sitting down to a nice dinner right about now, confident that he's got us bottled up good in Caldwell," I told them.

"Bon appetit."

Chapter Twenty-five

The road emptied out into the main road well beyond the point where Martin had his men posted. From that time on, traveling was fairly easy, with a full moon lighting the way.

The first night we camped was kind of strained, what with only one woman in camp with three men. Jerri slept on one side of the fire, while two of us slept on the other side, and one of us kept watch. Wyatt took the first watch, and Bat the second. Jerri insisted on taking her turn, so we set her up to go last. When I woke her up for her final watch I sat with her a while, on her request.

"Unless you're very tired," she added.

"No, I'm not that tired. Let's sit."

"I wondered how this would work," she said as we sat. "I mean, only one woman in camp—'"

"That won't pose a problem, Jerri. Believe me."

"I know, I know that now. They seem like nice boys—nice men. Bat seems just about my age."

"He is, but he thinks older."

"I can see that. Which one killed Jerry?" she asked.

"Does it matter?"

113

Um, no, I guess not—not really. It's just that—"

"It's just that he was your brother," I finished for her.

"Yes, I guess that's it."

We remained silent for a while and then I asked a question I had been thinking about.

"Jerri, about your brother, Jerry. Did he—I mean, was he ever, uh—"

"You mean, did he ever use me, like the others?" she asked.

"That's what I mean, yeah."

"No, Jerry never did. You know, he was Pa's black sheep because he wouldn't stay around and lick Pa's boots like the others, you know? But in some way, Jerry was more decent than the others."

I looked doubtful, and she hurriedly added, "I mean, he was a thief, and probably a killer, but he never touched me the way the others did. I don't know why, but—"

"Did you love him?"

She thought that one over a moment.

"I guess if I loved any of them, it was Jerry," she said, then she stopped and thought it over one more time. "No, I guess I didn't love him—not now, anyway. As kids, we really got along, then when Pa and the others started using me, things changed between me and Jerry. He wouldn't use me, but he wouldn't come near me, either. Maybe he thought I was dirty, or something. I don't know, things just changed between us, and then he went away."

"Did you ever hear from him?"

She shook her head.

"No, never. He was gone two years and I never heard from him."

"He never wrote?"

She laughed.

"He didn't know how to write."

"A rich man like Bull Martin, and he didn't send his kids to school to learn to read and write. Isn't one of your brothers a lawyer, or something?"

"Beau, he's the oldest. He's a lawyer, but all he handles are Pa's affairs. Pa won't let him go off on his own. He won't let any of them—of us—go off on our own. Except for Jerry. Jerry refused to go to school, that's why he couldn't read or write."

"How did your father feel about Jerry?"

"Angry, hurt—"

"Did he love him?"

She ran her fingers through her long hair as she thought about that one.

"I don't know if he loves any of his children," she answered. "That wouldn't matter, though, whether he loved Jerry or not. He was still his son, and the man who killed him will still have to pay for it. That's the way Pa is."

"Family man, huh?"

"Sounds funny, doesn't it? That's what he was, though, in his own way."

"Yeah."

We sat quiet for a while and then I said, "I think I'll turn in for a couple of hours. You okay?"

"I'm fine. As long as I'm along I want to pull my own weight," she answered.

I patted her shoulder and then went to my bedroll.

Was I just naturally suspicious? Was that why I'd asked all the questions about her brother Jerry? Did she love him? If she did, she'd want his killer, and that's why she was along. Either that, or she just wanted to get away from her family—if you could call it that.

I thought I had stopped being suspicious of her, and maybe I had reason to stop, but I always did have a suspicious nature. It comes from a long career as a lawman, when people just naturally lie to you.

If she was lying to me, she was a natural.

Chapter Twenty-six

At one point during our travels we had paired off, with Wyatt and me riding about ten feet behind of Bat and Jerri. They were talking together, but we couldn't make out what they were saying.

"You watch her like a hawk," Wyatt commented all of a sudden.

"Huh?" I asked.

"Jerri, the little bull," he said. "You've been watching her ever since we started out."

"You noticed."

"Don't you trust her?"

"I'm not sure, but it doesn't do any harm to keep an eye on her," I replied.

"I guess not. Did she love her brother, do you think?"

I thought about telling Wyatt just what being part of Bull Martin's family had meant for her, but decided not to. Revealing that was her business.

"She says not," I answered. "She says she might have loved him when they were kids, but that she hasn't seen or heard from him in two years."

"That doesn't mean that she doesn't love him."

"I know that."

"If we have to watch her while we're watching for them," Wyatt said, "that will make things that much more difficult for us."

"True, but she was right about one thing."

"What's that?"

I looked at Wyatt and said, "If and when Bull catches up to us, she may come in handy."

He nodded his agreement, and we rode on ahead to catch up to Bat and Jerri.

As we rode up next to them Jerri turned to Wyatt and said, "You and Bat are both from large families, he tells me."

"That's right."

"And you have none?" she asked me.

"No. I've never known what it's like to have any family, let alone brothers and sisters."

"Why is that?" Bat asked, suddenly interested in my past. He was interested, but I wasn't. Not any more.

"That's something I don't talk about," I replied. "I'd like you to understand that. I don't talk about my past with anybody."

Wyatt watched me with no expression on his face. Bat looked openly curious, but didn't ask anymore questions. Jerri frowned, studying me in a puzzled way, but she too didn't ask anymore questions.

That killed conversation for a while and we rode that way, four abreast, into Texas, where new dangers were ahead of us.

This was Comanche country.

Chapter Twenty-seven

In the past I'd had a few run-ins with Indians, and one memorable one with the Comanches. I was not, however, an authority on Indians by any stretch of the imagination. Still, I was able to tell when we were being followed, and when I realized this I let Wyatt and Bat know without letting Jerri find out.

"Why did we ride through Indian country, anyway?" Bat asked.

"It might change Bull Martin's mind about following us," I answered.

"Or, at least, some of his men might turn back," Wyatt added.

"But if we don't live through it, it won't matter if they turn back or not," Bat said.

"Painfully true," I said.

"What are you three talking about?" Jerri asked.

"Indians," I called ahead, and with a sidelong glance at Wyatt and Bat I went on, "and what to do if we run into any."

"Well, come and tell me, too," she asked.

I rode up to trot alongside her and explained what I knew—which wasn't a whole lot.

"The most important thing is not to show fear," I told her. "The Indians respect courage, especially the Comanches."

"How do they like white women?" she asked.

I hesitated a moment, then said, "Medium rare, I think."

"You louse."

"Just remember, you can be scared, but don't show it."

"I've had plenty of practice at that," she said, but elaborated no further. I thought I knew what she meant.

I had turned my head a couple of times, catching sight of two different braves. As far as I knew beyond that, there could have been two or twenty, but they were on our trail, watching and waiting. Maybe they thought we were going to meet someone and wanted to wait until there was a larger group and something to steal. Or maybe they just wanted to play with our nerves, to see if we'd give any sign of fear.

I had instructed Wyatt and Bat not to look back under any circumstances. If we all started looking over our shoulders, they'd think we were afraid. That would be like waving a red flag under a bull's nose. The longer we feigned indifference, the longer we'd stay alive.

My part was the most important. I was the oldest one of the four. Wyatt was only twenty-four, while Bat and Jerri were still in their teens. As capable and competent as they all were, they would still look to me for guidance—although Bat and Wyatt would probably never admit that. Still, I felt that I had to set the example and show no concern over the fact that Indians were on our tail.

To that end, I began to whistle.

That's when they came.

"Shit," I said, looking over my shoulder.

"What's wrong?" Wyatt asked. I pointed, and they all looked.

There had to be about twenty of them, and they came over a rise riding fast and screaming at the tops of their lungs.

"Let's move!" I shouted, and we took off as well.

"But don't look scared, right?" Jerri shouted.

"Shit," I said again to myself, and kicked Duke's ribs. "Let's go, big boy!"

Chapter Twenty-eight

"Think we lost them?" Wyatt asked, squinting his eyes in an effort to see how far behind us the Indians now were.

I turned in my saddle and looked behind us myself, saying, "I think we outran them. Lost them? Not likely. Hopefully, we discouraged them a little."

"We've got to give these animals a breather," Bat said, coming up alongside us.

I checked their three mounts and they were blowing up a storm, their sides swelling with the effort to catch their breaths. Duke, on the other hand, was breathing slightly hard, and could have gone on for miles yet. By the time he was ready to stop, the other mounts would have dropped dead.

"Okay, let's take a break and give them a chance to catch their breath," I agreed.

We dismounted and bunched the horses together.

"Should we take off their saddles?" Jerri asked.

"No," I answered, "we may have to move out in a hurry. We'll just let them rest a while."

Their horses were lathered up pretty good, and tired, but they'd given a good account of themselves in trying to keep up with Duke, and keep ahead of the Indians. I think it was their desire to keep up with Duke that had enabled us all to outrun the Indian ponies. Instead of them holding the big guy back, he had in effect carried them along.

"That horse of yours looks like he was out for a light trot," Bat commented, admiringly.

"He's got a lot left," I replied.

"Have you ever really let him out?"

"Once or twice. I've never seen anything on four feet move as fast as he can, or for as long. He's one of a kind."

"I can believe that."

Wyatt was sitting on a large rock, keeping watch behind us, so the Comanches wouldn't be able to sneak up on us.

"See anything?" I asked.

"Not even dust."

"What could they have been after?" Jerri asked.

"Who knows?" I answered. "It could have been you, or it could even have been Duke."

"It didn't have to be anything in particular," Bat offered. "Maybe they just wanted blood."

"Savages," Jerri said, which I thought was an odd remark coming from a girl whose family had treated her the way they did.

I went over to Duke and, patting his neck, started telling him how great he was. He likes to hear it every once in a while.

Jerri came up to me and asked, "How long before we get into New Mexico?"

I looked up and answered, "If we hadn't had to

push the horses we might have made it by nightfall. Now we may have to wait until tomorrow. We'll see how long a rest we need."

She nodded and touched Duke's nose, stroking it. He stood still and tolerated her touch. I hadn't seen him react favorably to the touch of many people other than myself.

"Anything, Wyatt?" I heard Bat call out.

"Nothing."

"They must have given up, Clint," Bat said to me. "We discouraged the hell out of them."

"Looks that way," I agreed, watching Jerri Martin the whole time. She looked like she had something on her mind.

"Having second thoughts, Jerri?" I asked her.

"What?" she asked, as if she hadn't heard me. I'd obviously snapped her out of her reverie, and now she looked at me and said, "No, no second thoughts." Then she smiled and said, "I'm way past that now. I'm up to fifth and sixth thoughts by now, but I'm still not going back."

"Good girl."

I went over and checked out Wyatt's mount for him while he was standing watch. He seemed to be okay, having regained his breath. None of the horses showed any signs of damage from the long, hard run from the Comanches.

"They look good," I told Bat. "I think we can get going now. We might make New Mexico by nightfall. There's a small town we can spend the night in if we get that far."

"Sounds good to me," he answered, and went to get Wyatt.

"Still no sign of anything," Wyatt told us,

mounting his horse again. We all mounted up and I took the lead.

The next stop was a little town called Little Domingo, New Mexico.

Chapter Twenty-nine

We were about a half hour out of Little Domingo when night fell, and we all voted to keep going. By the time we finally rode into the little New Mexico town, we were all ready for some food and some rest.

"Why don't you three go in and see if we can get something to eat?" I suggested. "I'll take the horses to the livery and put them up for the night."

Everyone agreed, so I left them in front of the saloon and took the horses over to the stable.

As always, I paid some extra money to have Duke taken special care of, but before I left I gave in to my suspicious mind and searched Jerri's saddlebags. I didn't know what I was looking for, but I knew I'd found something when I found the letter. It was dated a month earlier, and it was from Jerry Martin. I didn't read it right away, but tucked it away for later on. Just the fact that it was there told me that she had lied to me at least about being in contact with her brother. She'd insisted that he didn't even know how to read and write. Granted, the handwriting on the envelope was somewhat childish, but it was legible.

With the letter in my pocket I walked to the

saloon and found the three of them at a back table.

"Any chance of some food?" I asked them.

"Little girl said we could get some beef stew and bread, but that was all," Wyatt told me.

"A little girl?"

"If she's a little girl," Jerri said laughing, "I don't know what that makes me. She's bigger and older than I am."

"Not by much, though," Wyatt told her, and we all laughed.

"I'll take stew as long as I can get three beers with it," I said.

As if on cue, the bartender came over with four mugs of beer and set them down in the middle of the table.

"Thanks," I said gratefully, and we all reached and drank deeply—even Jerri. When the food came and we began to eat it became apparent that Jerri had an appetite that would shame many men twice her size. The stew was warm instead of hot, and the bread was hard, but the beer was cold and we were hungry, so it all went.

The "little girl" Wyatt had been talking about turned out to be a girl of about his own age, who was about five-four with a healthy bosom and a slim waist. She flirted with Wyatt throughout the meal, and before we were done it was obvious where he was going to spend the night.

After dinner we agreed that we should leave at first light, so Wyatt stood up and said, "That don't give me much time, so I better get started now."

He walked over to the girl—whose name was Luz—whispered in her ear, and then they went upstairs together.

Wyatt was a fast worker with the ladies when he wanted to be, but just as quickly Bat produced a deck of cards and had a four-handed poker game going with some of the locals.

"Sure you don't want to sit in?" he asked me.

"Maybe later," I answered, and he went and got the game underway.

"You could have played," Jerri told me when we were sitting at the table alone. "Don't feel you have to pay me any attention. I can find my own amusement."

"Oh, really?" I asked. "Like what?"

"Like sleep. I haven't ridden this far in—well, I've never ridden this far or this hard, and I'm bushed."

"Why don't I walk you over to the hotel?" I asked her.

"What about Bat and Wyatt? Should we get them rooms?"

I looked at Bat, who was already raking in a pot.

"They can fend for themselves," I answered. "Come on, I'll walk you over."

During the walk to the hotel she told me, "Clint, don't feel you owe me anything, okay? I'm just riding with you, like Wyatt and Bat. I don't want any special treatment."

"Walking a lady to her hotel does not come under the heading of special treatment in my book," I explained. "It's the same thing I'd do for any lady."

"Do you really think I'm a lady?" she asked.

"Yes, you are a lady, Jerri. Just because you can ride and shoot, that doesn't make you any less a woman."

That pleased her and her walk acquired a bit more spring from then on.

At the hotel I asked for and got two rooms. When I handed her the key to hers, she looked at me strangely, but took it without a word. She was probably wondering why I didn't just get one room for the two of us, but probably put it down to more "lady" treatment. At least, I hoped she did.

When I left her at her door she asked, "Do you want to come in?"

"No, Jerri. I want to go over to the livery and check on the horses. I want to make sure they're all in good shape for tomorrow," I explained.

"Oh. Well, okay. If you want to come in later, just let me know, all right?" she said, obviously disappointed.

"I will. Why don't you get some sleep. You need it."

"Sure. Good night."

"Good night."

The reason I wanted a separate room was so I could read her letter in privacy. I walked down the hall and opened my door as quietly as possible, so she wouldn't know I was going into my room. Once inside I sat on the bed and took out the letter.

It was a disappointment. It read:

Will get money soon, then you can leave.
See you soon.

Jerry 1

The handwriting was barely legible, but that didn't change the fact that she had lied to me. For all I knew, this was just the most recent of many letters. If it was the first in two years, it didn't make much sense. The way I read it, Jerry 1 meant he was the oldest of the two, making her Jerry 2. Probably something that carried over from childhood. I also figured that he was trying to get some money to either send her or bring her, so she could leave home.

Would a brother do that for a sister he didn't love, or who didn't love him?

If she loved him, why was she traveling with us, the men who killed him? Could she really forgive and forget that easily? Was she really just taking advantage of a chance to get away from a family who had abused her for years? Or was she planning something, some kind of revenge? What could a little girl do against the three of us? I wondered.

Chapter Thirty

I left my room as quietly as I had entered and went back downstairs.

"The girl I came in with," I asked the desk clerk. "Did she leave the hotel?"

"No, not that I saw," the young guy told me. He was young enough to have noticed her if she had come down the steps.

"Thanks."

I was fairly certain Jerri was still in her room. I went back to the livery stable, as I had told her I was going to do, only not to check the horses. I went back to return the letter, so she wouldn't notice it was missing. It was virtually all she had in there of any personal value. The rest was supplies we had bought for the trip. She was still wearing the clothes she had on when we left, as the rest of us were. When we reached a larger town we'd worry about more clothing, and possibly baths.

My main worry was Jerri, and what her plans were. She'd had every opportunity to kill us in our sleep when it was her watch, and she hadn't done it. What was she waiting for? What sort of revenge could she possibly have in mind that she'd pass up a chance to kill us?

Maybe I was worrying about that part of it too much. The only thing I should have been thinking about was the possibility that she lied to me at least once. I'd been watching her closely the whole way; I was just going to have to watch her even closer. That meant not letting her take a watch alone, but not letting her know that I was suspicious of her. I couldn't very well stay awake every night during my watch and hers, so I was going to have to let Wyatt and Bat know about it.

"Checking yer animals and yer gear?" the livery man asked. "This here's a nice town, Mister. Don't nobody steal nothing don't belong to 'em."

"I was just looking for something. I must have dropped it on the trail. Take care of that big guy extra special, okay?"

"You got it, Mister. Animal like that deserves special treatment."

"Thanks."

I went over to the saloon, where Bat was still busy taking money from the locals.

"We have to talk," I said over his shoulder.

"In a while."

"Now, and then you can go back to your game, I said, more urgently. He looked up at me, saw that I meant it, and slid back his chair.

"Excuse me a moment, gentlemen. I'll be right back."

He got up and we walked to another table and sat down.

"What's up? Those three are just aching to hand me as much money as they got," he said.

"You can go back in a minute," I said, and went

on to explain about Jerri and her brother.

"So she lied," he said when I was finished.

"Yes."

"Why don't we just cut her loose, go on without her?" he asked.

"Because there's a possibility I may be wrong. Also, if she's got something on her mind, it might be better if we have her where we can see her. All we got to do is keep an eye on her, and not let her know it."

"That means pulling double watches."

"That's right. We'll split them up."

He thought it over, then agreed.

"Can I go back to my game now?"

"Sure. Don't lose too much, okay?"

"That'll be the day. You going up to tell Wyatt, now?"

"Yup."

"Likely to catch him in mid stroke, you know," he warned.

"I want to make sure we all know what's going on."

"Where's the little bull?"

"In her hotel room."

"You got separate rooms?"

"Yeah. I wanted to be able to read her letter without her looking over my shoulder."

"Yeah, well, back to the fish."

I asked the bartender what room Luz was in and he told me. He also told me she was occupied. I told him it was all right, because the fella she was occupied with was a friend of mine, and we shared most everything. He gave me a strange look and I headed for the stairs.

I found her door and knocked. When I didn't get any answer, I turned the knob and walked in.

The first thing I saw was one of the shapliest behinds I've ever had the pleasure to see. It was pumping up and down with increasing speed and I leaned against the wall and waited until there were two great groans of relief and pleasure.

"Nicely done," I said, complimenting them both.

The girl sat up and turned in my direction, a surprised look on her face. Wyatt leaned his head to one side to see who it was. When he saw me he smiled and said, "Hi, Clint. Didn't know you were the kind who liked to watch."

Fact of the matter was, I didn't like to watch, but couldn't avoid the fact that watching had gotten me some excited. The girl climbed off Wyatt and sat next to him, and the sight of her heavy, pendulous breasts with their dark, hard nipples excited me all the more.

"What brings you up here if it ain't watching?" he asked.

"I could be nice to your friend too, if you like," Luz offered, leaning against Wyatt's shoulder.

"What do you say, Clint?" Wyatt asked.

"No thanks." I didn't like watching, but I disliked sharing even more. Besides, as long as Jerri was along and I had to watch her close, you couldn't get any closer than being in the same bed, could you?

"I just want to talk to you for a minute, Wyatt. If you could slip your pants on and step out into the hall?"

"Sure," he said, swinging his feet to the floor.

"Hurry back," Luz called after him as he pulled his pants on and walked towards me. "I am not yet satisfied."

Outside he said, "That little girl might kill me before morning."

I told him about a little girl who might just be planning to do that somewhere along the way.

"What could she possibly do to the three of us?" he asked.

"I don't know. That's the only flaw in my thinking, but it won't hurt to keep an eye on her just the same."

"I agree, but if you don't mind, there's another little girl who is waiting for me to put more than my eye on her. Why don't you go back to the hotel and do the same to the little bull? You couldn't watch her any closer than that."

"I've already thought of that, Wyatt," I assured him. "I've already thought of that."

Chapter Thirty-one

"I've been waiting for you," Jerri told me as I entered her room. The door had been left unlocked for me.

She was kneeling on the bed, with the moonlight coming through the window and falling on her. She looked very young and incapable of killing a man, unless it was in bed. Those beautiful breasts looked rock hard and firm in the moonlight, although I knew they would yield to the touch of my hand.

"Undress," she said to me. "Hurry, please."

I undressed and approached the bed and she reached for me with eager hands.

"On the trail I'd look at you and want you, want to touch you and have you touch me." I grasped her breasts and she held her breath and said, "Yes, like that." I touched her further down with my other hand and she moaned and said, "And like that, yes, just like that."

I lowered her onto her back and got in bed with her. I began running my lips over her shoulders and breasts, biting her nipples, sucking on them until she took hold of my head and pushed it into the warmth of her breasts, moaning and calling my name. With my other hand I sank first one finger, then another into the steaming depths of her and she began to buck, lifting her hips to meet the pressure of my hand. She reached down with her left hand and took hold of my erection, began kneading the length of it.

"I want this, oh how I want this," she whispered to me.

Never one to deny a lady what she wanted, I raised myself above her and allowed her to take hold of me and guide me into her.

"Oh, yes," she breathed in my ear. "Yes, oh yes."

Her body was smooth and warm beneath me, but she was powerful for a girl her size. She locked her legs around me and I started to stroke her, slowly at first, and then faster until her nails were raking my back and she was tossing her head from side to side, biting her lip. Afraid she might bite through her lower lip I kissed her, parting her lips and plunging my tongue into her mouth. She sucked on it furiously as I continued to stroke her, and then bit it when she climaxed, almost hard enough to draw blood.

I reached around and grabbed her buttocks, driving deeper as I climaxed and emptied myself into her. Her heels began to drum on my behind and she covered my face with kisses, ending with a deep, burning kiss that bruised both of our mouths.

"Oh, yes," she said when the spasms had subsided in both of us. As I started to withdraw she cried, "No, please, stay in me," and grabbed my buttocks with both hands.

She was vulnerable at that moment, and I was tempted to ask her point-blank why she had lied to me, but thought better of it. I didn't want to alert her to the fact that I knew she had lied. There might be a better time and place.

"More," she said, "please. More. It has to last until next time, and who knows when that will be?"

Who even knew if there would be a next time?

As she began to move her hips in a way designed to bring me back to an appropriate hardness, I wondered if that very thought wasn't going through her mind as well, but for a different reason.

Maybe she was planning on this being the last time, and wanted to get every drop of satisfaction that she could.

Chapter Thirty-two

First light found us all ready to leave. I'd spent the night with Jerri, sleeping fitfully, waiting for her to plunge a knife in my back, but she had chosen to pass up another excellent chance to kill me.

Wyatt looked a little worse for wear. Luz hadn't killed him, but she'd taken a lot out of him, that was for sure.

Bat looked fresh and eager to get moving. I didn't know where he had spent the night. Could have been at the poker table for all I knew, but he seemed well rested enough, and had added a few dollars to his poke.

"We ready?" I asked. We all were, so we moved out, with me in the lead.

We kept Jerri between us at all times, never letting her lag behind. On occasion we'd let her take the lead, but that was it. She was always in sight of one of us.

When we came to a large, steep, rocky slope we decided to go around it rather than risk injury to one of the horses. As we started around a volley of shots came and Bat went flying from his horse.

"Take cover!" I shouted. I jumped off Duke and

139

slapped him on the rump. He kept running, out of harm's way. The other horses ran off in different directions. Wyatt and I had thought to grab our rifles first, and Bat hadn't a chance to. Jerri apparently hadn't been able to think that quickly, but her sixgun was in her hand before she hit the ground.

As she took cover, Wyatt and I came up alongside Bat and we each grabbed an arm and pulled him to safety behind some rocks.

"How bad?" I asked.

Wyatt turned Bat over to look, but it was Bat himself who answered.

"High on the shoulder," he said. "I'm sure it went right through."

Wyatt produced a neckerchief and plugged the hole as best he could.

"Can you shoot?" I asked Bat.

His wound was on his left shoulder, and I hadn't noticed that his gun was already in his right hand.

"I couldn't grab my rifle as I fell," he lamented.

"Don't worry about it." I peered up the slope and said, "Let's see if we can find out where the shots came from, and how many men we're dealing with."

. I looked to my right and saw Jerri behind another large rock.

"I'm going to draw their fire," I told Wyatt. "See if you can figure out how many, and where they are."

"Right."

"Okay, ready. Go!" I shouted, and took off.

I ran as hard as I could over to where Jerri was and the shots started again. I dove head first and rolled to where she was.

"Are you all right?" she asked anxiously.

"I'm fine," I told her. I looked over to Wyatt and called out, "Did you get it?"

He held up three fingers and said, "Three, more than halfway up the slope."

I nodded, then leaned on the rock we were behind and looked up the slope.

"Do you see them?" Jerri asked.

"I think so," I answered. I thought I could make out two of them, but couldn't locate the third.

"They've got us pinned down," she said.

"Yes, it looks that way. We're going to have to work our way up the slope towards them. If we start to get too close they might break off and run for it."

"And we might end up dead."

I looked at her and said, "Not you, Jerri. Me, and Wyatt. We're going to work our way up while you and Bat lay down some cover fire."

"How's Bat?"

"He's okay. He's got a hole high on his shoulder. We've stopped the bleeding. I'm going back over to Wyatt now to tell him our plan. Cover me."

"Right."

"Ready? Now!"

She started firing up the slope and I took off back to where Wyatt and Bat were. They were firing upslope also, so the barrage directed at me this time was not as dense as last time.

"Okay," I told Wyatt and Bat, "we've got to get up that slope. Wyatt, you and I will try it while Bat and Jerri lay down cover fire."

"Right," Wyatt agreed.

"We've got to force them to break off and run," I told Wyatt. To Bat I said, "Bat, you're going to have to watch Jerri as well. If she chooses to fire at Wyatt and me instead of those men up the slope, we'll be caught in a cross fire. You'll have to take care of her, then."

He didn't look particularly happy about the possibility of shooting a woman, but he said, "Don't worry."

"We can't afford to worry about what's going on behind us," I replied. "You ready, Wyatt?"

"I'm ready."

"If one of us gets hit, the other will have to keep going."

"Right."

"Let's go then. Ready . . . now!"

We started up the slope, widening the distance between us as we went. Lead started flying all around us, up and down the slope, but we kept as low as we could and kept going. I kept waiting for one of Jerri's shots to take me in the back, but she was either a bad shot or she was really laying down cover fire.

We made it part way up the slope and found cover. I checked Wyatt and he signaled that he was all right. Neither one of us had been hit, and that was lucky. I looked up the slope and I could see the three of them now. They were peering over their cover, trying to locate Wyatt and me. I signaled Wyatt, and we started up again.

My hat went flying off me backward, plucked off by a shot from above, not behind. I thought I felt something tug at my upper left arm, but kept going.

Again we found cover, and we had halved the distance between us and the riflemen. I glanced at my left arm and saw that I was bleeding, but it was only a crease. I looked over at Wyatt and saw him tying a piece of his shirt sleeve around his left hand. When he was finished he signaled that he was okay.

Up the slope things were getting nervous. They were shouting back and forth, and then two of them began firing while one started to work his way up the slope. Wyatt and I both fired, and the man went down. Bat and Jerri started firing, and apparently the two remaining men did not like the odds. Instead of one covering the other, they both decided to run, and they both died for it. We all stopped firing, and when it was obvious that the three men were not going to move, we started cautiously up the slope.

When we reached them they were all dead. I turned and motioned to Bat and Jerri to come on up.

"Let's turn them over," I suggested. We rolled the three of them over on their backs.

"Recognize any of them?" I asked Wyatt.

"No, not a one," he replied.

The one that we had both fired at had two bullets in him. The other two had been hit once and twice respectively.

"How's your hand?" I asked.

He looked down at it, then unwrapped the piece of shirt from it.

"Creased the back," he replied. "It's stopped bleeding already."

As had the crease on my arm. We were lucky that the damage was so minimal, and that the three men were apparently lousy shots.

Bat and Jerri reached us, and Bat sat down on a large rock.

"You okay?" I asked.

"A little weak, but I'm okay," he replied.

"Jerri, why don't you take a look at these three?" I suggested.

"All right."

She holstered her gun and walked over to examine the three dead men.

"Recognize any of them?" I asked.

I watched her as she inspected the faces of each man, and then she turned to face us.

"I recognize them, all right," she answered. "They're all from my father's ranch."

That just confused me more about Jerri Martin. Asking her if she recognized any of the men was my way of testing her, because I had already recognized one of them.

The first man we killed had been Post, the man who had found us in the Caldwell livery stable.

Chapter Thirty-three

"Should we bury them?" Jerri asked.

"No," I said. "Wyatt, let's get their horses and see if there's anything on them we can use. Jerri, see what you can do about Bat's shoulder."

Wyatt and I started up the slope, but Jerri grabbed my arm.

"Okay, but isn't this just a little like stealing from the dead?" she asked.

"No, it's not," I answered, "because the dead can't own anything. They're dead."

Wyatt and I went up the slope and located the three dead man's horses. We went through their gear and came up with some useful supplies, like coffee, bacon and beans.

"Their guns?" Wyatt asked.

I thought a moment, then decided not to take them. If I'd had my rig with me I would have. They wouldn't have been a burden then. "Leave them."

"What about our horses?"

I pointed down the slope and he looked. Duke was trotting to the base, and behind him were the other three animals.

"I don't believe it," Wyatt said.

"Believe it," I replied. "They won't move again unless he does. Let's go."

We went back down to where Jerri had finished patching up Bat's shoulder.

"I did the best I could," she said as we approached.

"She did fine," Bat agreed. He stood up, probably just to show us he could.

"Why don't you just sit back down there until we're ready to go?" I said. He nodded and sat down.

"Let's see what they've got," I said to Wyatt, indicating the dead men.

I didn't find anything on the first man that was worth keeping, but when I searched Post it was a different story.

"Nothing on the other one," Wyatt said. "What have you got there?"

"Post was carrying this in a shoulder rig," I told him, showing him the gun I was holding in my hand.

It was a brand new gun introduced by Colt, a .22 caliber New Line Special. It was light and only 57mm long, just right for a shoulder rig, only what was a cowboy like Post doing with it?

Wyatt took it from me and checked it out.

"Holds seven shots," he commented, turning it over in his hand. "It's kind of small, isn't it?"

"That's the beauty of it," I said, taking it back. "Small and light, but in the right hands, just as lethal as a forty-four."

"You want the shoulder rig?" he asked.

"No, just the gun," I said, tucking it into my belt. "Let's get reloaded and get going. We'll hole up somewhere ahead and talk about what this means."

"Bat, you ready to go?" Wyatt asked.

"Sure, let's ride," Bat replied, standing up. His spirit was more willing than his body was. He wasn't that steady on his feet.

"We'll find a doctor soon, Bat," I promised him.

"I'm fine," he insisted. "Come on, let's go."

We worked our way down the slope, with Wyatt staying by Bat, to steady him. I let Jerri go down ahead of me, wanting to keep her in front of me in spite of the way things had gone with her. I had more food for thought about her as a result of the attempt at bushwhacking us.

She'd had a chance to shoot either Wyatt or myself in the back, and claim it was a mistake, or to deny recognizing any of the three dead men. She hadn't done any of those things. Why the hell not?

Chapter Thirty-four

We made camp a few hours later, in a gully we could cover pretty well. Bat was getting a little feverish, and we eased him off of his horse and laid him down.

"I'm fine," he kept insisting, but the beads of perspiration on his forehead told a different story.

I handed Jerri a canteen and told her, "See what you can do to make him comfortable."

"Okay, Clint."

While she was doing that I went up to where Wyatt was keeping watch and sat with him.

"What do you think?" Wyatt asked.

"I don't know," I admitted. "How the hell did they get ahead of us?"

Wyatt shrugged. "Somebody talked."

"Who? Jerri? She's been with us all the time."

"In town, before we left?"

"She didn't know where we were going," I pointed out.

"What about Nathan, the bartender. Sometimes, we even forgot he was around. Maybe we said too much in front of him."

"Maybe."

I tried to think back. Had we mentioned our

route around him? And if we had, would he have told Bull Martin?

"Okay, let's forget about who talked, for now," I decided. "If they got here ahead of us, they could even be further ahead of us. Where do we go from here?"

The question hung in the air for a moment, and the answer came from an unexpected source.

"I say keep going," Jerri's voice said from behind us.

We both turned to look at her, and then beyond her to where Bat lay.

"He's asleep," she informed us, knowing what we were thinking. "It's not a bad wound, but there's a danger of infection. He needs a doctor."

We both knew she was right about that.

"That's one reason why I say keep going. Are we closer to a town going forward than we are going back?"

"Yes," I said.

"And I think you're both wondering who talked, who told Post and the other two men you—we—would be coming this way. You might even think I told someone—like my father."

Wyatt and I exchanged guilty looks.

"My father is not a fool, Clint, and he had enough men to send three east, three west, three north or three south, hoping they'd cross paths with you."

"Would he tell them to shoot on sight, even if you were with us?"

"I don't think so. I think Post resented what happened in Caldwell and wanted to get his revenge."

"So then where's your father?" I asked.

"Probably in Caldwell, waiting for a telegraph message that you've been seen somewhere."

"Okay, so if what Jerri says is true," Wyatt said, "changing direction could bring us right into the arms of another group of Bull Martin's men. If that's the case, then that's another reason to keep going straight ahead."

I looked over at Bat and said, "The first thing we've got to worry about is getting Bat to a doctor. Agreed?"

"Agreed," Wyatt said.

"Okay with me," Jerri said.

"Jerri, why don't you go sit by him, in case he wants something?" I suggested.

She looked at both our faces and then said, "Okay."

When she was gone Wyatt said, "She feels we might be suspicious of her now, I guess."

"Yeah, but only just now, because of the bushwhackers. My test didn't work, Wyatt."

"You mean asking her if she recognized those men, giving her another chance to lie?"

"Yup. You heard what she just said. She knew one of the men was Post. I forgot for a minute that she was in that livery with me."

"That could be another indication for her that we don't exactly trust her," he suggested.

"Yeah, if she catches on."

Wyatt looked up and said, "We got daylight left, Clint. What's the closest town?"

"If we cut south we could make Zuni Flats by nightfall," I said.

"But?" he asked, hearing it in my voice.

"Indian country."

"Zuni?"

"No, years ago, maybe. Apache country, now."

"Well, we went through Comanche country, didn't we?" he asked.

"Sure, when we were all healthy and able to ride hard. We're going to have to go easy with Bat, but we could still make it by nightfall."

"They got a doctor?"

"Shit, I hope so. I'd hate to make the trip for nothing."

Chapter Thirty-five

We headed for Zuni Flats, keeping our pace slow so as not to bounce Bat around too badly.

"Too slow," Bat said at one point.

"What?" Wyatt asked.

"We're going too slow," he said again.

"We're fine," I called out. "We'll make it before nightfall."

"Bullshit," Bat said viciously, and kicked his horse into a gallop.

"That crazy—" Wyatt shouted. "He'll fall off!"

"I'll get him," I called out. "Don't run your mounts!"

I knew I could catch him with Duke, so there was no point in Wyatt and Jerri spending their horses.

"Let's go get him, big boy," I told him, and we took off.

Bat was holding on, but I knew the longer he ran his horse like that the better chance he had of opening his wound. If he fell off, he could hurt himself even worse.

I hoped I could reach him in time.

"Bat, pull up!" I shouted when I got near

enough that I thought he might hear me.

I caught up to him just as he was slipping off his horse. I drew alongside of him and kept him from falling, then pulled up his mount.

"That was a dumb stunt!" I snapped at him.

He looked at me with a mixture of anger and chagrin. "I know it, damnit!"

Wyatt and Jerri rode up on us at that point.

"You okay?" Wyatt asked Bat.

"I'm fine, I'm fine. I just didn't like the idea that I was slowing you down."

"You're slowing us down even more by pulling something like this," I said. "Now we've got to give your horse a chance to rest. Stand down so he can catch his breath."

Wyatt dismounted and helped Bat down.

"Clint," Jerri called out suddenly, and the tone of her voice made me look up quickly. She pointed behind us and I looked.

"What is it?" Wyatt asked, coming up alongside of me.

"Dust, and a lot of it," I said.

"More of Martin's men?"

"Or Apaches. Get Bat back on his horse, Wyatt. We've got no time to rest now."

We boosted Bat back on his horse and then mounted up ourselves.

"Get going!" I told them.

"What about you?" Wyatt asked.

"Whoever that is I've got to slow them down. We can't outrun them with Bat. You stay with him, make sure he stays on his horse."

"Clint, you can't—"

"I'll slow them down as much as I can, Wyatt.

Just keep going south, you'll come to Zuni Flats.
I'll join you later. Do what I tell you, damnit!"

"Good luck," he said. He wheeled his horse
around and pulled up alongside Bat, and then they
started off as fast as they could.

"Clint—" Jerri started, but I gave her no time.

"Move, Jerri!"

I pulled my rifle out and got ready to take on . . .
what?

Chapter Thirty-six

If there was someplace to hide, I would have hidden until I could see what I was up against, but the ground was flat as far as the eye could see. I just sat there atop Duke with the rifle resting on my knee, watching that cloud of dust getting closer and closer, while Wyatt, Bat, and Jerri's cloud kept getting farther away. When I was roughly equidistant from each cloud of dust, I started riding Duke back towards the advancing one.

As we got closer and closer to each other my hands started to sweat. I didn't know which I preferred, Bull Martin and his men, or the Apaches. At least the Indians wouldn't be motivated by revenge, only bloodlust. They might give up easier than Martin would. Then again, Martin would probably only kill me if he caught me.

Gradually the dust cloud began to take shape. Riders, four . . . five . . . at least six, maybe more.

And they were Indians.

I looked behind me and I was still able to make out the small dust cloud my three partners were kicking up. I was going to have to lead the Apaches in another direction.

But first I was going to make sure I caught their attention.

I stopped Duke and sat there, waiting, watching them get closer and closer. I knew when they spotted me, because they stopped also, and we sat there, not close enough to make out faces, but close enough to know who was who.

My first instinct was to take off, but what if they didn't follow? How long would they just sit there and watch if I didn't move at all? That was no good, either. What I had to do was get them to follow me away from the others.

I raised my rifle, sighted, and fired. A puff of dust kicked up about a foot in front of the lead rider, just as I intended.

That got their attention, and they started riding towards me at a fast clip. I could hear their war cries as they got closer and closer, and I waited until the last possible second before wheeling Duke to my left and taking off in a westerly direction.

The chase was on. They had gotten close enough to start firing, but whether they were unfamiliar with rifles, or just bad shots, none of them succeeded in hitting me or Duke, for which I was grateful.

I knew I could outrun them, but I held Duke in reserve, so I wouldn't discourage them too soon. Occasionally one or two of them snapped off a shot, but the distance between us was widening, and they didn't come close. Then things went wrong. I was about to let Duke go flat out when he stepped in a hole and we went down.

I kept my head, held onto my rifle. I rolled with

the fall and came up on one knee. My first thought was for Duke, and how badly he was hurt, but he had gotten back to his feet and was apparently all right. Then and only then did I check to see how close the Apaches were.

They were thirty yards way and closing fast. The smart thing would have been to lay Duke down and use him for cover. If that was the smart thing, then what I did was dumb, because I stood up, slapped him on the big rump and yelled, "Get out of here!"

I dropped to one knee again and began firing as fast as I could lever a new round into the chamber. There were more than I had originally thought, because I knocked three of them from their horses and there were still at least six closing in on me.

"Shit," I said out loud as they bore down on me, some firing rifles, the others arrows. I rolled to my right and kept rolling as they rode over the spot where I had been kneeling. As they went past me I took two more from their horses. I worked the lever two more times before I realized the rifle was empty. As they turned to come back at me I pulled my revolver from the holster, and the .22 from my waist. I fired with both hands as they came back, and by the time both guns were empty, one brave was left, riding down on me.

He launched himself off his horse and landed on top of me, and the knife in his hand sliced along my left side. The blood began to soak through my shirt and I fought to get out from under him. By the time I got him off and then turned him over, I saw that he was dead, with three little holes in his chest from that little .22 New Line.

I was out of rounds for the gun, now, but it had served its purpose well.

That little gun had saved my life.

Chapter Thirty-seven

When all the fireworks were over Duke came back and nuzzled me while I sat on the ground, trying to stop the bleeding in my side.

"Come here, big guy," I told him. I checked his right foreleg, which was the one that had gone in the hole. There wasn't any obvious damage, and he was able to rest his considerable weight on it, so the damage, if any, was minimal. I turned my attention to myself.

The damage to my side was really not all that bad, it was just placed so as to make it difficult to stop the bleeding. I stanched the wound with a bandanna.

Not wanting to push Duke too early, I decided to walk him a bit before finally mounting up and riding for Zuni Flats.

"Jesus," I said, as the movement of riding caused a burning pain in my side. I took to riding with my hand plastered against the cut, but it was next to useless. Eventually I started to feel very weak and doubtful of my ability to stay in the saddle all the way to town.

"Duke, pal, if I pass out it's up to you to get us

there," I said to him. "Don't let me down, old friend—at least, not until we get to Zuni Flats."

I thought that when I finally fell off Duke's back somebody was catching me and lowering me gently to the ground.

I just hoped it wasn't any of the wrong people.

Chapter Thirty-eight

Awareness was at first elusive, and then came suddenly.

"It's about time," a voice said, and I turned my head to the right and found Jerri sitting at my side.

"For a while we didn't think you were going to make it back," she told me. "Then when you finally got here we didn't think you were ever going to wake up."

"How's Duke?" I asked with a dry throat.

"That's your first thought?" she asked. "Your horse?"

"My partner," I corrected, "and he got me here, didn't he?"

"He sure did. You were just hanging onto the saddlehorn letting him do all the work. He's got a bruised right foreleg, but other than that he's fine."

"What about Bat?"

"He's okay, too. We got him here and to a doctor before any infection could set in. Now do you want to know how you are?"

"I guess."

"The doctor stitched up your side, but you lost a lot of blood. He said that was why you passed out in the saddle, and he doesn't know how the hell you managed to stay on a horse. Then there's your head."

"Is it still there?"

"You had a nasty gash, but he closed that up without stitches."

"Must've hit my head when we fell."

"Do you want to tell me what happened now?"

"Why don't you get Bat and Wyatt, so I don't have to tell it twice?" I suggested.

"I'll get the doctor, too," she said, getting up from her chair.

"Good idea."

When she left I moved myself around experimentally. The side was taped up, and itched a bit. There was a small bandage on my forehead and my head was hammering. Everything else seemed to be in proper working condition.

Twelve Apaches, I thought, that's how many there had been. Had they been riding fanned out, I might have run a lot sooner and tried to outdistance them a little faster. The way they had been riding I hadn't thought there were that many. Also, if it hadn't been for that .22 caliber New Line, I'd probably be dead. I wouldn't have had time to reload, and one or more of those braves certainly would have gotten to me, instead of just one making a last ditch try at me before dying.

I looked around the room, saw my gunbelt hanging on a chair, and the .22 sitting on a dresser. I was shirtless, but was still wearing my pants. At my feet were my boots, and when I bent to pick them up and put them on, the world tipped over and I almost fell off.

"I don't think that's at all wise."

I waited until my vision got back to normal then looked at the man standing in the doorway.

"You the doctor?" I asked.

"I am. Doctor Ruiz, at your service. I would suggest that you elevate your feet once again and lie back in bed. It shouldn't be too long before you will be able to get up, but give it a few more hours. Let me check your wounds."

I lay back and he approached the bed and began fiddling with my bandages.

"Where are my friends?"

"They are coming. Señorita Smith is going for them now."

"Señorita Smith?" I asked.

"Si. Lie still, please."

Well, someone had been smart enough not to use Jerri's real name, just in case Bull Martin's fame had spread this far south.

"How is my friend?" I asked.

"You mean Mr. Masterson? A flesh wound, I assure you. It was wise of all of you to get him to a doctor before the wound became infected. He will be fine."

"Is he up and around?"

"Si, he is a stubborn one, but he is so young he can afford to be."

The doctor was in his forties, with a high forehead, a tiny mustache, and delicate hands. He probed my side, causing me to wince just a bit.

"The cut was not too deep," he said, "but you will be sore for some time."

"Can I sit a horse?"

"Surely, if you wish to open the wound again.

Señor, you must be content to stay with us for a couple of days, at least, just to allow the wound to begin to heal. Then you may travel."

"We don't have a few days," I said, as he probed the cut on my forehead.

"How many fingers do I hold up, Señor?" he asked, holding up three—I hoped.

"Three."

He nodded, keeping the accuracy of my guess to himself.

"You and your friends, you are—how do you say, on the dodge?" he asked.

I hesitated a moment, wondering if his question was just idle curiosity.

"Let's just say that we're trying to keep one step ahead of somebody."

"The law?"

"No," I said, shaking my head and then regretting it, "not from the law, of that I can assure you."

He regarded me for a moment, then sat back in his chair and said, "All right."

At that point Jerri came in, trailed by Wyatt and Bat.

"How's the patient, Doc?" Wyatt asked.

"He will be fine if you can convince him he should stay off his feet until morning, and that he must stay in town for a few days before trying to travel."

Wyatt looked at me and I shook my head, indicating that now was not the time to discuss the merits of that suggestion.

"May we speak alone, Doctor?" I asked.

"Of course," he said, rising and walking to the

door. "You know where to find me—although you should not have to, if you follow my instructions." To Bat he said, "You should be off your feet also, my young friend."

When he left I said to Bat, "Don't worry, you have an excuse."

"What is it?"

"The doctor says you're young enough to be stubborn."

He laughed and approached the bed.

"This is the man who was telling me about dumb stunts, huh?" he asked.

"Yeah, well, we're all entitled to one of those," I replied.

"Want to tell us what happened?" Wyatt asked.

I went through it step by step, up until I couldn't remember anymore, and then Wyatt took over.

"Your horse came walking into town with you hanging on somehow. We were watching for you, and got to you before you could hit the ground."

"I appreciate that."

"After that the doctor took over."

"How long—do you have any whisky?" I asked, changing my priorities in mid-sentence.

"Over here," Jerri said. She walked to the dresser and took a bottle from one of the drawers.

"No glass," she apologized.

"Just hand it here." I took off the top and took a long, greedy swallow. It burned down to my stomach and I shuddered for a moment, then I took another swallow and started to feel alive.

"How long ago?" I asked.

"You've been in town about six hours," Wyatt said.

"And the doctor says we should stay a few days more," I told them. "What do you think?"

"Well, he told Bat the same thing, but he's ready to ride," Wyatt said.

"But Clint's not," Jerri argued. "If he tries to ride he'll open his wound."

"You all go ahead, I'll stay behind."

"I'll stay with you," Jerri said.

Wyatt and Bat exchanged glances and Wyatt said, "We'll all wait until we can leave together."

"Has this town got a telegraph office?" I asked.

"Yes," Wyatt answered, and we all let that hang in the air for a while. I killed the time by working on the bottle again.

"Okay," Bat said, breaking the silence, "so somebody could send a telegraph to Bull Martin, but who would?"

"The doctor?" Jerri suggested.

"He asks a lot of questions," I pointed out.

"I think he's just curious," Wyatt said.

"Maybe," I said.

"Look, get some rest," Wyatt said, "and let Bat and me think it over for a while. We'll let you know what we come up with. Okay?"

I started to reply, then stopped. I'd been making most of the plans up until that point, just naturally doing so because I was the oldest. Maybe it was time to let them make some.

"All right," I agreed.

"I'll stay with him," Jerri said, starting for the chair by the bed.

Bat grabbed her by one arm, and Wyatt took the other and said, "We said rest, Jerri, real rest, okay?"

She shook them off and gave them both a dirty look, but when they left so did she.

I finished off the bottle and fell asleep.

Chapter Thirty-nine

"Okay, this is what we came up with," Wyatt told me the following morning. "About ten miles west of here there's a town, a small town·that's dead now."

"A ghost town?"

"I guess you could call it that. No one lives there anymore. Me and Bat, we figure we can ride over there and hole up until you and him heal proper. Also, if Martin catches up to us, nobody else will get caught in the crossfire. We'll take enough food and supplies to last us a while, settle in and see what happens."

I thought it over and couldn't see anything wrong with it.

"I've also sent some telegraph messages of my own. Oklahoma, Kansas, Missouri—"

"What for?"

"Help. My brothers, Morgan and Virgil, are traveling. My message should catch up with them."

"You told them where we are, where we will be?" I asked.

"Martin would find us anyway, Clint. We all know that now. It's time to stop running and fight, only we're picking the place."

He was right about one thing. Running wasn't our style. We'd tried it, and it didn't work, so yes, it was time to stand and fight.

"Well, let's hope your brothers get to us before Martin. We could use the help."

"Bat sent a message to his brother, Ed, too."

"Fine, when they get here they'll be six of us," I commented.

"Seven," he corrected. "Jerri says she'll stay with us. That is, she'll stay with you."

"Stubborn, huh?"

"Like a woman."

"I'll talk to her. She'll be safer on the other side, with her old man."

"Sure," he said.

There was a question to be asked, and we let it lie for a while until it grew too big to keep in.

"Has she been near the telegraph office?" I asked.

"One of us has been with her all the time," Wyatt told me.

"All the time?" I asked.

For a moment he looked guilty, staring at the floor.

"Forget it, Wyatt. I'll talk to her. Meanwhile, stock up for the move."

"We'll get a buckboard. You and Bat can even ride in it."

"Somebody's got to drive it, right?" I asked.

"Yeah. What kind of shells you need?"

I told him what I needed for my handgun and rifle, and then what I needed for the .22.

"It's new, so that may be hard to get, but see

what they've got, huh?"

"Sure."

"Any place where we can get a good breakfast?"
I asked, "I'm starved."

"Downstairs is pretty good. We ate already, so
you go ahead while we get things ready. Want me
to walk you down?"

"Wait a minute."

I stood up, testing my legs and my balance.
When I didn't fall over I told him, "I'll be all right.
Go ahead."

"I'll see you later."

After a large breakfast I felt a lot better, except
for the itch in my side from the bandages. When I
walked out onto the street I saw the buckboard in
front of the general store, and Duke was tied to the
back of it along with Bat's horse.

"Hiya, big guy," I said, stroking Duke's neck.
"Saved my neck again, didn't you?"

I untied his lead from the back of the wagon because it wasn't necessary. He'd go where I went
without that.

Wyatt came out of the store followed by Bat and
Jerri.

"You ready, Clint?" he asked.

"I am if you are," I answered. I walked over to
Jerri and said, "Jerri—"

"Forget it, Clint," she said. "They both already
tried. I'm going with you," she said, then louder,
"with the three of you."

I looked at Wyatt and Bat and said, "Stubborn."

"Like a woman," Wyatt said.

Chapter Forty

"Ghost town is putting it kindly," I said as we entered the town that would be our home for a while.

I spotted a sign over the old hotel that said: DEAD-MAN FLATS.

"Appropriate, don't you think?"

"Jesus," Wyatt said. "Nobody told me the name of the damned place."

"It doesn't matter," I replied. "A rose by any other name. . ."

"Think they've got any vacancies?" Bat asked. He was on his horse, testing his wound as we neared the town. I had stayed on the buckboard, because I knew if I sat a horse I'd bust open the stitches the doctor had worked so hard putting in.

"I'll check out the hotel," I said. "Wyatt, you and Bat look the town over. No use in finding any surprises later."

"Right."

"What about me?" Jerri asked.

"You? Why don't you get us something to eat?"

"I'm not—"

"You wanted to come along," I told her. "Looks like you're going to end up being the cook. You

171

can cook, can't you?"

"Better than you can shoot," she snapped back.

"Looks like we're in for some fine eating, Bat," Wyatt said so she could hear, then he and Bat went off to check around.

"Let's check out the hotel," I told her. "Maybe they've got a stove, we can eat and sleep in the same building."

"All right."

As we entered the hotel I was going to keep her with me every step, and then thought better of it. Might as well let her pull her own weight. That was what she wanted right from the beginning.

"Jerri, check down here, see if they've got a kitchen. I'll check around upstairs."

"Right."

I went up and checked out the rooms. It was a small hotel, with only two floors, and only the second floor had rooms. From the looks of things, travelers had made use of the premises from time to time, but at the moment no one else was there.

Coming back down I found Jerri at the front desk.

"Last entry is dated 1869," she said. "This town has been dead for a long time."

"No guests right now, either."

"Except us."

"And we're not going to sign the register. Find a kitchen?"

She nodded. "And a stove. All we need is some wood."

"We'll get some. Let's bring some of the gear in."

I carried in most of the small, less heavy stuff,

careful of my stitches the whole time. Jerri carried in a few heavy items I wouldn't have thought her capable of carrying. When Wyatt and Bat returned, they brought in the rest of the stuff.

"I'll take a front room," Wyatt said, "and Bat will take one in the rear, this way we can see trouble whichever way it comes."

"Good idea," I said. "One of us will have to keep watch at all times, probably from the roof. This appears to be the highest building in town."

"It is," Wyatt verified. "All of the others are empty, Clint, and have been that way for a long time."

"This appears to be the popular building," I told him. "Anytime anyone drifts into this town, they hole up here. Wyatt, Jerri needs some wood, and since Bat and I are, uh—"

"I get it. I'm the only able-bodied man, huh? You sure you and Bat didn't plan this? I'll get the wood."

"Good, then I can get started cooking," Jerri said.

"And the sooner she cooks, the sooner we eat," I said.

"Okay, I'm going, I'm going," Wyatt said.

"I'll get on the roof," Bat announced, picking up his rifle.

"I'll relieve you so you can eat," Wyatt told him.

"And I'll take a turn." They started to argue but I said, "If Bat can, I can. Besides, what is there to do but sit. I'll take a chair up with me."

While everyone got busy, I started checking the guns and the ammo.

I checked the rifles, all but Bat's, which he had

taken on the roof with him. In checking the ammo, I found a couple of boxes of .22 caliber shells. The gun wouldn't do very much at long range, but if we got in tight, I was glad to have some shells for it. I took it from my belt, loaded it, then replaced it.

Wyatt came in with an armful of wood that looked like it came off the side of one of the buildings.

"It's just lying all over," he said, "for the picking."

"I hope we don't end up burning the whole town in that stove," I told him.

He walked through into the kitchen to give Jerri the wood, then came back out.

I handed him his rifle. "You keep this thing in good condition."

"Thanks. I got you some shells for that .22."

"I saw, thanks," I said, touching it. "This baby saved my life once already. Its earned its keep."

"I'm going to take another walk around town," he said. "See if I can find anything that might be useful."

"Okay."

As he left I could smell burning wood, and then I heard the sizzle of frying bacon. I went into the kitchen and watched Jerri working around the stove.

"Hey, you really do know how to cook, don't you?" I asked her.

She turned to face me and said, "You could make yourself useful and peel some potatoes."

"I guess I could do that."

I took up a knife and began peeling.

"Jerri, why did you lie to me?" I asked, the question out of my mouth before I even realized I was going to ask it.

She turned her head and stared at me with her mouth open.

"About what?"

"About having heard from your brother. I found that letter from him in your saddlebag."

She dropped the utensils she was holding and demanded, "What right did you have to go through my saddlebags?"

"The right of a man who wants to stay alive, angel. You mean I shouldn't have been suspicious of the daughter of the man who wants to kill me?"

She stared at me for a long moment, then went back to what she was doing.

"All right," she said over her shoulder.

"All right, what?"

"You had a right to be suspicious."

"So then answer my question. Why did you lie to me?"

She stopped what she was doing again, but kept her back turned to me.

"All right, I admit it," she said finally.

"Admit what?"

"My reason for wanting to come with you," she answered.

"Which was?"

She turned around violently now, the knife she was holding held straight out in front of her.

"I wanted to find the man who killed my brother, and kill him!"

Chapter Forty-one

"Do you still feel that way?" I asked her.

"I don't know. I'm all confused now."

"You had quite a few opportunities to take your revenge, you know," I told her.

"I know it."

"Maybe you just couldn't do it, even if you still wanted to."

"Yeah, maybe."

"And you still don't know which one of us killed him, right?" I asked.

"Right," she said, and then she snapped, "I don't want to know!" and turned back to the stove.

"Okay, why don't you just finish making us something to eat? I'll see you in a little while."

"Where are you going?"

"I just want to look around and check on Duke."

When I got outside the buckboard and horses were gone. I assumed Wyatt had taken them to the livery stable and went off in search of it.

"Clint," I heard Wyatt call. I turned and saw him standing in the doorway of a store across the street. I walked over to him.

"You moved the horses, I hope."

He smiled and said, "Yeah. I put the buckboard in the livery, which is right around the corner, but I've got the horses in here."

"In here?"

"Sure, take a look."

I followed him in. A large chunk of the rear wall had been knocked out, somehow, and he had led the horses in that way.

"If they get past us," he reasoned, "the first place they're going to look is the stable, for the horses."

"And they'll be in here. It's good, Wyatt, a good idea."

"Yeah, I thought so."

"I just spoke to Jerri about lying to me."

"Do you think that was wise, tipping her off like that?" he asked, looking doubtful.

"Actually, the question was out of my mouth before I even realized it."

"What'd she say?"

"Not much. She admits her original aim was to kill whichever one of us killed her brother, but now she's confused. I don't really think she'd be capable of doing it, in any case. Not in cold blood."

"I agree."

"We'll keep watching her, just in case, though."

"I agree with that, too."

"Okay, I'm just going to look after Duke, and then I'll see you inside."

"Right."

I checked Duke's legs and hooves, then brushed him some and gave him some of the oats we brought along.

"You're a good-looking devil, Duke," I told him. "Sometimes I'm almost sorry I gelded you. You should be glad, though," I went on, patting his neck. "You never have to deal with the female of your kind. God knows, the female of my kind are a confusing lot." I started away and gave him a parting pat on his hind quarters. "Be grateful, big buddy. I saved you a lot of headaches."

Now if I could only save myself some, that would be an accomplishment.

Chapter Forty-two

For five days we passed the time playing poker, first two-handed, with the third man always on the roof, and Jerri watching. Eventually she got tired of just watching and we started to teach her how to play. Her beginner's luck was phenomenal, but after a couple of days things evened out and she began to lose her winnings at a steady rate.

We were playing for two bits, and four.

We also began to get on one another's nerves, which is the way people get when they're cooped up together. Having three men with one woman didn't help, either.

Passing her around would have been too much like what her family used to do with her, so she made her choice, and she chose to spend her nights with me. I thought that it might have been a blow to Wyatt's ego, since it was obvious that she had spent that one night in Zuni Flats with him.

On the fourth night, when she came to my room, I had decided that it would be for the last time. By the time this was all over, either we'd be dead, or other members of her family would be, possibly even her father. I didn't think she would be able to overlook that.

As she rode my rigid erection up and down, her head thrown back, her muscles clenching and unclenching, I fingered her marvelous breasts, saying goodbye to them, goodbye to the hard, brown nipples, to the firm, smooth skin.

When her body shuddered with her orgasm I squeezed her breasts hard enough to leave the imprints of my fingers, and emptied myself into her.

Then I told her what I'd decided.

"But, why?" she asked.

"There's too much tension here as it is, Jerri. We're getting on each other's nerves, and your coming to my room every night doesn't help. We've got to stop."

"But Clint, you must know that the only reason I stayed—" she began, but I didn't let her say it.

"We've got to stop, Jerri. When your father catches up to us, you're free to go out to him before the shooting starts."

She gave me a hurt look, then stood up and put on her clothes. Her parting look was no longer hurt, but cold.

"Maybe I'll do just that, Clint Adams," she said, and left, slamming the door behind her. A short time later I heard the door to her room slam, even louder.

In the morning she didn't speak a word to me as she served up breakfast to me and Wyatt. Bat was on the roof. I'd go up and relieve him after I'd eaten.

Both of our wounds had begun to heal fairly well and we were both moving about almost normally.

When I went up to the roof to relieve him, he was grateful.

"I'm starved," he told me.

"At least we're eating well while we're cooped up," I replied.

"Sleeping well, too, for the most part," he said, "except for last night."

"Last night?"

"What with door slamming, and feet stomping. Did you and Jerri have a falling out?"

"I told her not to come to my room anymore. It only adds to the tension."

"What if she chooses to go to Wyatt's room tonight?" he asked.

"That's between her and Wyatt, Bat. It wouldn't bother me. Would it bother you?"

"Not me."

"She might even come to your room," I added.

He smiled, saying, "Hell, that wouldn't bother me, either. See you later."

Three hours later Wyatt came up to relieve me.

"Jerri doesn't seem too happy today," he commented. "She hasn't said a word to any of us today."

I told him what I had told Bat.

"You didn't have to do that, Clint," he said afterward.

"It doesn't matter, Wyatt. I have the feeling that we won't be here much longer."

"How's that?"

I pointed to the north, and he looked. He could see it just as well as I.

"A dust cloud," he said.

"Made by more than a few riders."

"My brothers?"

"Your brothers, even if they had met up with

Bat's brother, would still only be three riders. They wouldn't raise a cloud of that size. No, it's Indians, or Bull Martin."

Chapter Forty-three

We started alternating the guard every two hours after that. From the beginning we had not allowed Jerri to take a turn. We told her it was because she was doing all the cooking, which she seemed to accept. Whether or not she questioned the reason in her own mind was unknown to us.

"How far away do you think they were?" she asked me during a poker session between us and Bat.

"They wouldn't be able to make it here by nightfall. They'll have to hold up somewhere for the night. They should be here by morning."

"By morning," she repeated.

Bat bluffed her out of a pot and she got angry and stalked out of the hotel.

"Where do you think she's off to?" he asked, shuffling the cards.

"Probably just for a walk. If she goes for the horses, Wyatt will see her."

"Unless she goes in through the back. She could scatter the horses, and then we'd be stuck." He put the cards down and said, "Maybe I'll just take a walk, too."

"It wouldn't hurt," I said, and he got up and followed her out.

I set up a solitaire game and began to think about alternatives.

If we knew who was out there, exactly who was coming, we'd know how to set up for them. The best thing to do would be for one of us to ride out at dusk and scout whoever was coming. Whichever of us went could be back by morning and then we'd be able to get ready.

I carefully stacked the deck the way I wanted it, and then put it aside.

I stood by the front door until I saw Bat and Jerri coming back together. Jerri did not seem as tense, and Bat looked a little cocky. I thought I could pretty much figure out what had happened between them.

Jerri walked past me without a word and went into the kitchen. Bat came in and stood beside me, watching her. Then he turned to me and smiled, saying, "She didn't wait until tonight."

I wondered if Wyatt had seen them from the roof.

Chapter Forty-four

"So we'll cut the cards to see which one takes the ride," I proposed.

"Fair enough," Bat said. Wyatt also nodded his agreement. We let Jerri take a turn on the roof while we had discussed it. Nothing would happen before morning, anyway.

I let Bat walk over and get the cards and place them on the table before us. It was just a chance that he wouldn't shuffle them first; and he didn't.

Bat drew a King, with his customary luck.

Wyatt didn't do badly, drawing a Jack.

I fingered the carefully stacked deck, and produced an Ace of Spades.

"If I didn't know you better," Wyatt said, dropping his card on the table, "I'd be tempted to think you stacked the deck."

"Then it's a good thing you know me," I replied. "Let's have a drink, and then I'll go and saddle Duke."

Bat went and got a bottle of whisky and we had one drink.

"You fellas try and get along while I'm gone, huh?" I told them.

"You try to get back in one piece," Wyatt replied.

"I'll see you in the morning," I said, putting down my empty glass.

It was almost dark by the time I got Duke saddled and rode out of Deadman Flats.

I had to judge roughly the path of the dust cloud we had seen, and ride for it, hoping I didn't bypass them. If I got out too far I wouldn't be able to make it back by morning.

The last thing I wanted to do was get back too late.

When I had ridden a couple of hours I slowed Duke down to a walk, mindful that sounds carried at night. I held my rifle across my lap and kept as alert as possible. I had some jerky along with me and chewed it just to stay awake. I tuned my senses to smells especially, and that was what finally told me I was getting close: the odor of coffee and frying bacon led me right to them.

I dismounted, keeping my rifle with me, and went the rest of the way on foot. The land was so flat here that there was nowhere to hide, so I got down on my belly. I knew there was no danger of Duke giving me away, because he'd remain quiet and still until I returned.

They apparently had no fear of being discovered, because they had posted no guard. I got close enough to their fire to be able to make out their faces in the flickering light.

You couldn't mistake the face of Bull Martin, sitting right there in the center. Apparently he hadn't been able to hold onto all his boys, or else the rest were still scattered about. He had with him his four sons, and five other men.

Ten against three, not counting Jerri on either side. She still wasn't sure which side she was on. When the time came that she'd have to decide.

They were talking, and I settled down to listen.

"Pa, what we gonna do about Jerri?" Wes Martin asked.

Bull Martin dumped the remains of his coffee onto the fire, causing it to sizzle and dance, and then said, "That'll be up to her, boy."

"We need her back, Pa," he said.

"We know why you need her back," Jim Martin spoke up. "No other woman would let the likes of you touch her."

"Shut up," Bull snapped.

"Let's quit this fighting among ourselves," another man spoke up. From the looks of him, and the way he spoke, I took this to be Beau Martin. "It's not serving any good purpose."

"Listen to him talk fancy," Ben Martin drawled.

"He talks smart, too," Bull said, "like I wish the rest of you boys could."

"Aw, Pa, you're always puttin' us down," Wes complained.

"Can you think of any good reason why I shouldn't—you especially. You're the dumbest sonofabitch I ever did see."

The others laughed, and Bull added, "The rest of you ain't much better, neither. Beau here is right. Stop fightin' among yourselves. They'll be plenty of fightin' for you tomorrow."

"And killin'," Wes said.

"Yes, and killin'."

"We gonna kill them all, Pa. All three men, I mean?" Jim asked.

"I want that young one, that Masterson," Ben

spoke up. "Fancy Dan thinks he's a hotshot card player."

"How do you know that?" Bull Martin asked quickly.

"I jes heard tell, Pa," Ben hedged. Apparently he hadn't told his father about his trip to town to play poker.

"Ben, I ever find you went into that town—I always wondered how you knew about this Bat Masterson being with them."

"Pa, I tole you, I jes heard tell."

"Yeah, you told me."

"So, we gonna kill them all, or what?"

"We're gonna kill them that killed your brother," Bull answered. "If this Masterson fella gets in the way, he gets killed, too. That plain enough for you?"

"And what about Jerri?" Beau asked.

Bull seemed to take the question more seriously since it was coming from his eldest—and smartest.

"We won't hurt her if we don't have to," he said finally.

"She's pretty handy with that sixshooter," Wes said.

"You heard Pa," Beau said. "Don't hurt her. You men better get some sleep," he said, speaking louder for all to hear, "we'll break camp at day-break."

There was a lot of commotion in camp at that point, as men scurried to set themselves up comfortably by the fire, and I took advantage of it to back off and make my way back to Duke. For a few moments there I'd been tempted to pick off a couple of them—Bull and Beau, since they were the brains, and maybe Jim—but I decided against it. I wasn't ready to trade their lives for mine.

I thought I was worth ten of each of them, and that was without exaggeration.

Chapter Forty-five

I made it back to Deadman Flats by daybreak, and Bat waved at me from the roof of the hotel. Inside, the smell of fresh coffee made my mouth water.

Wyatt was sitting at the table, just getting ready to eat his eggs, bacon, and potatoes. When he saw me he stood up and smiled.

"Well, glad to see you back."

"Shit, that coffee smells good."

"Here, sit down," he said, moving away from his chair. "Jerri," he called out, "Clint's back. Make up another plate for me, will you?" To me he said, "You eat this one and I'll tend to your horse. Don't worry, I'll take good care of him. Come on."

"Thanks," I said. I took his chair and hungrily swallowed a mouthful of eggs. Jerri came out at that point and put a cup of coffee down in front of me.

"Thanks, Jerri," I said, looking at her.

She hesitated a moment, then said, "I'm glad you made it back," and went back to the kitchen.

By the time Wyatt had returned I was finished with breakfast and working on my second cup of coffee. Bat came downstairs and Jerri came from the kitchen. They all looked at me expectantly.

"Well?" Wyatt finally asked.

I looked at Jerri, then back at Wyatt when I said, "It's them."

"Pa?" Jerri asked.

"And your brothers."

"And how many others?" Bat asked.

"Ten all told, maybe a dozen. They were breaking camp at daybreak so they should be here before noon, if they ride hard."

"We'll be ready," Bat said. "I better get back on the roof, just in case they decided to leave earlier. We don't want any surprises."

"Bat, why don't you keep the roof? Wyatt, you take the roof across the street."

"Shouldn't we all stay in one building?"

"I think we'd be more effective if we could keep up some kind of a crossfire. Is there a stairway on that building across the street?"

Wyatt shook his head. "It fell a long time ago."

"Then they won't be able to get at you up there very easily."

"There's a stairway in back of this building," Jerri pointed out.

"If I'm reading Clint right, there won't be by the time he and I are through."

"Right. We've got to make ourselves as inaccessible as possible. I'll stay down here to keep them from getting in. Jerri, you'll be at the back window down here."

She wasn't likely to see anyone there for a while. They'd probably try taking us from the front first. I was keeping her out of the way, delaying her decision as to whether or not she'd fire on her family.

I went around behind the front desk where I had the boxes of extra shells stacked. I threw one to Bat and he went on up to the roof. Wyatt came over, picked up his rifle and an extra box of shells.

"Let's get the stairway taken care of," he told me.

We went out back and, using large, already fallen pieces of wood like sledgehammers, we demolished the back stairway of the hotel.

"I'll get up on that roof across the street," he said. It was the same building we had the horses hidden in.

"Wyatt, did you tie Duke to anything?"

"Yes, I did."

"Do me a favor and untie him. If they get in there I want him to have a chance to get away."

"Right."

"Leave the rest of them tied. The shooting might spook them and we'd lose them anyway."

"Okay."

I went back inside and set my rifle and a box of shells by the front window. Jerri did the same at the back.

"Clint?"

"Yes?"

"What if I can't shoot?" she asked.

I turned and looked at her. "If you can't shoot, it will be because you can't shoot to kill. Shoot over their heads if you have to, just keep them away from the back of the hotel. Make noise, Jerri, that's all I ask."

"Okay," she agreed. "I can do that."

"Good girl."

"I'll make more coffee."

"Jerri?"

"Yes?"

"My offer still stands, you know. When they show up you're free to go out to them. I heard your father say he didn't want you to be hurt," I said, leaving out the part where he said, "If we don't have to."

She stared at me, obviously still undecided.

"Any time you decide, you let me know," I said. "They'll let you come out."

"I'll—I'll . . . make some more coffee," she said, and went back to the kitchen.

She had a hard decision to make, and I realized that it could go one of three ways. She could stay with us. She could go out to them. And she could change her mind entirely, and shoot me in the back, avenging her dead brother.

Chapter Forty-six

Bat and I went through two pots of coffee, with Jerri bringing him his up on the roof. It was too risky to send her across the street to Wyatt, so he had to make do with a canteen and a bottle of whisky.

I kept my eyes on Wyatt most of the time. He'd give me a signal when they were close enough to see.

Jerri was making more coffee when Wyatt finally waved down to me and disappeared from sight.

"Jerri?"

"Yes?" she called from the kitchen. Just from that one word and the way her voice shook, I knew she was scared.

"It's time."

"All right."

I moved to the door and stuck my head out far enough to see the beginning of Main Street, which we were on. I watched until my eyes started to burn, and they finally came into sight.

Bull Martin was right up front, flanked by his boys, Beau and Jim. The others were fanned out behind him, and an accurate count made it eleven men altogether.

I went back inside and took up my position at the window, rifle in hand.

"Adams!" Bull Martin's voice boomed out.

I didn't answer.

"Clint Adams!" he called out again.

He either wanted to talk, or wanted to locate us. I assumed he wanted to talk, and decided to give him his answer.

"Adams!" he called a third time.

"I'm here!" I called back. I saw his head move as he sought the direction of my voice.

"Send my daughter out, Adams," he called out.

I turned around and looked at Jerri, who shook her head at me solemnly.

"She's free to come out if she wants to, Bull," I called back to him. "She doesn't want to."

"I don't believe that," he said. "I want to talk to her. I want to see her."

I turned to her and she put her rifle down and walked to the door.

"Remember," I told her, keeping down as I spoke. "It's your choice."

"Pa!" she called, stepping outside. She kept walking until she was in the middle of the street.

"Come on, Jerri. We'll cover you," he told her.

"I'm not leaving, Pa. Not unless you promise to leave them be," she called out to him.

"What are you talking about, girl?" he demanded. "Them varmints killed your brother, don't you understand that?"

"I understand what kind of man Jerry was, Pa, better than you do. I believe they had no choice—"

"That don't matter, girl!" Bull shouted vehemently. "He was still my blood, your kin!

They killed him!"

"I'm blood, too, Pa. You gonna kill me if I don't come out? I don't want these men killed, Pa!"

There was a movement behind Bull, and I saw the flash of a gun. It was Wes, with a gun in his hand. I was about to fire at him when Bull reached back, swung at his son and said something to him. Wes touched his face where his father had struck him, and holstered his gun.

"Girl, I'm going to give you time to think it over. You got one hour, Geraldine Martin, and then if you don't come out, I'll go over you if I have to. The choice is yours!"

He wheeled his horse around and the others did likewise, and they rode away.

I stepped out into the street and shouted up at Wyatt, "How far away did they go?"

"Not far. Just out of earshot. They've circled their horses and the old man got down."

I waved at him, then walked to where Jerri stood, crying.

"Jerri—" I said, touching her arm. She didn't move, didn't make a sound. She just stood there as great big tears worked their way down her face to her chin, where they dropped off, making even bigger wet spots in the sand.

"Jerri, I'll saddle your horse, and you can go out to them. That's the best thing for you."

"And what's best for you?" she asked, "And Wyatt and Bat? To stay here and get slaughtered? How do you think I'd feel, sitting out there and watching them kill you?"

"How will you feel being in here with us as we kill them?"

She swiveled her head around and stared at me, mass confusion plain in her eyes.

"Honey, this is our choice. We don't want to be running forever. We are choosing to fight, and we've chosen the spot. If we're going to die, at least it was our choice. You've got to make a choice, Jerri. You can't die because of indecision. Make a choice and live with it . . . or die with it."

She took a deep breath and turned her head, looking out at where her father and brothers were waiting. Then she looked back at me, took another deep, shuddering breath, and made her decision.

She walked back into the hotel, picked up her rifle, and took her place at the back window.

Chapter Forty-seven

After half an hour of Bull Martin's alloted hour went by, I suddenly began to wonder if Wyatt and Bat knew what was going on, if they were able to hear what he had said from all the way down the street. I hoped neither one of them would start anything until the hour was up.

"Jerri."

"Yes?"

"Will you be all right down here for a couple of minutes? I want to make sure Bat knows why we're waiting."

"You don't think he heard?"

"He might not have been able to hear from up there. I'll be right back down."

"Sure, go ahead."

I squeezed her shoulder and then went up to the roof.

"Whoa," I said when Bat turned towards me with the rifle.

"Jesus, I didn't hear you. You move like a cat."

"Sorry, I just wanted to make sure you knew what was going on. Could you hear their conversation from up here?"

"Jerri and Bull? Just snatches."

"He's given her an hour to make up her mind about which side she wants to be on. That was a half hour ago."

"Has she decided?"

"She only needed one minute," I replied. "When she walked back into the hotel with me, that was her decision."

"Poor kid. You think she's being honest now?"

"You do, don't you?"

"Yes."

"So do I. Wyatt won't fire until you do, right?"

"He said he'd keep watching me, since we couldn't get to him to let him know what was going on."

"Okay, good. I've got to get back downstairs. Good luck, and shoot straight."

"Is there any other way?" he asked.

"Not for us," I replied.

"Everything okay?" Jerri asked when I returned downstairs.

"Everything's fine, Jerri. How about you?"

"I'm fine, Clint. For the first time in my life, I really think I'm fine. I really know what I want to do."

"I'm glad. I wish the circumstances were different, but I'm glad, anyway."

"The circumstances are what forced me to make a decision," she told me.

"I know, I know. Why don't you go back to the rear window. We don't want them sneaking up on us."

"Pa won't let them make a move until the hour is up," she assured me, but she went back to the window anyway.

There was fifteen minutes left, and then some kind of action was sure to start.

In fifteen minutes there would be a lot of lead flying, a lot of blood flowing, and a lot of dead men. I was desperately trying to think of a way of stopping it.

"Jerri?"

"Yes, Clint?"

"Your brother Ben, he fancies himself a gunman, doesn't he?"

"Yeah."

"Is he any good?"

"Nobody's as good as he thinks he is," she said, "except maybe Wild Bill."

"Is he the best your father has?"

"Not if Stitch came with him."

"Stitch McCord is on your father's payroll?" I asked.

"Yes, he is. Do you know him?"

"I know of him," I replied.

Stitch McCord was considered by some to be in a class with the likes of Hickok, Thompson, and Wes Hardin as far as handling a gun. He was thirty-five, and had carried that reputation for about ten years now. There were stories that he had once forced Ben Thompson to back down from a gunfight, but knowing Ben I didn't believe that to be true. Some gunmen have found it necessary to spread rumors about their own prowess with a gun to enhance their own rep. Stitch McCord had always seemed to me to be that kind of a man. I doubted that he deserved to be mentioned in the same breath with Hickok, Thompson, or even the youngster, Wes Hardin.

I wondered how strongly Bull Martin felt about the abilities of McCord. It was obvious to me why McCord had hitched his wagon to Bull, and that was because I was involved. Being in on the death of The Gunsmith would be a feather in McCord's cap, and give some credence to his claims of being a fast gun.

I decided to give him that chance.

"Jerri, will you go out and give your father a message for me?" I asked suddenly, looking around for a white rag of some kind to use as a flag of truce.

"What message?" she asked, frowning.

I found something white and tied it to a long piece of wood. As I knotted it I told her what my proposal to Bull Martin was for putting an end to this business with as little bloodshed as possible.

"Clint, are you sure?" she asked in a low, serious voice.

"I think, if your Pa goes for it, it's the best thing for all of us," I told her.

"I don't know—"

I held the white flag out to her and said, "Come on, girl, let's put an end to this nonsense."

She hesitated, then took the flag and started out the door.

"Leave your guns," I called out. She stopped, leaned her rifle against the door frame, and dropped her handgun to the floor.

She walked out and I watched her walk to the center of the street. I wondered what Wyatt and Bat were thinking as they watched her walk towards her father. Surely they saw that she was unarmed, which would indicate that there was more involved than her going over to her father's side.

I moved to the door so I could see Jerri and her father, who stopped walking about ten feet from each other. They had a short conversation, and at one point Bull looked behind him for a moment, then turned back to Jerri, said something, and turned and walked away. Jerri turned and started back to the hotel.

"He agreed, Clint," she told me as she came back in, dropped the flag and picked up her weapons.

"But?"

"He's my Pa, but I don't know if I trust him. McCord will meet you out in the street, where me and my Pa were standing."

"Okay. Go up to the roof and tell Bat what's happening. Tell him to signal Wyatt to stand by."

"All right." She approached me and put her hand on my arm, saying, "Be careful, Clint. Don't trust them."

"Adams," a voice called. I looked out the window at a man I assumed was Stitch McCord. He was tall, lanky, wearing his gun on his left hip. "Come on, Adams, let's get this over with."

"I'm coming," I called out.

I eased the leather thong off the hammer of my gun and slid the revolver in and out of the holster a few times, to make sure it wouldn't stick. Then I stood up and walked out the door to meet Stitch McCord, one against one, his gun against mine, for all the chips.

Chapter Forty-eight

The message I had sent to Bull with Jerri was that I was the man who had killed his son, not Wyatt, and that I would face his best gun man to man. If I won, me and my friends would go free, including Jerri. If his man won, he'd have his revenge, and that would be that.

I could understand why Jerri didn't trust him, though. In either case, Wyatt, Bat and Jerri stood to go free, and Bull had agreed to that much too readily. If worse came to worse, at least I'd get Stitch out of the way, and losing his best gun might cause Bull to draw back, maybe give it up.

I walked towards Stitch McCord, who was standing with his feet spread, hand hanging limply by his holster. I was watching him, but I was also watching Bull Martin and the rest of his men, who were all on foot, themselves watching. I even thought I saw some money exchange hands, which meant there was some action being taken on this confrontation. I wondered what the odds were.

"Far enough, Gunsmith," McCord said. I was close enough to see his face, which appeared to be a map of scars and lines. McCord was just plain ugly, and that was a fact.

"I been waitin' for this ever since I signed on with this bunch," he said.

"This is a little out of your line, isn't it, Stitch?"

"What do you mean?"

"I mean facing a man, fair and square. That's not usually your style, is it?"

"You callin' me a back shooter? I ain't never backshot anybody," he said, with resentment. "Every man I ever killed I done fair and square."

"That ain't the way I heard it."

"I don't care how you heard it, I'm tellin' you the way it is," he snapped. He was getting angry, and I could see his left arm tensing up.

"All right, let's stop the talk and get on with it," I said.

"You'll see," he said. "You'll see."

He went for his gun and he was right, I did see. I saw very clearly, as if he were moving in slow motion. I had been right. McCord was nowhere near being in a class with Bill Hickok and Ben Thompson. He was second-rate at best.

There was something else I saw, however. I saw a signal from Bull Martin, and I saw ten other men also going for their guns.

Jerri had been right not to trust her father.

I didn't waste any time. I plugged McCord before his hand even reached his gun. The surprised look on his face would have been funny if I'd had time to savor it. As soon as I had fired I began rolling to my left, as chunks of lead were buried in the street where I had been standing.

From behind me I could hear Wyatt and Bat open fire. The ten men scurried for some kind of cover, and I did the same. I threw myself behind a long dry horse trough and a volley of shots pecked at the wood.

Suddenly, it got quiet, and I took the opportunity to reload the empty chambers in my gun.

I was effectively pinned where I was. If I raised my head above the trough the chances were good ten men were going to do their damnedest to shoot it off. I rolled over on my back and discovered that from where I was I could see Wyatt. I waved, to see if he saw me, and he waved back.

There was only one way for me to get back to the hotel and that was to run for it. I tried to convey my plans to him by hand signals, and he seemed to be nodding. I hoped we were reading each other right, and that he would convey the message to Bat as well.

I waited, and when Wyatt was looking straight at me, I waved, got up into a crouch, and then took off.

Lead flew in both directions, and the din was deafening. I ran for all I was worth, waiting for a chunk of hot lead to catch me in the back. As I dove through the door of the hotel and hit the floor I was surprised to find that I had made it cleanly—or so I thought. It wasn't until Jerri shouted, "You're hit!" that I realized she was right. There was blood on my left arm, but no pain yet.

"Shit," I said, because I knew that any second the pain would start. "Get a bottle of whisky!"

While she did that, I tore away the sleeve of my shirt to see how bad the wound was. It was a clean hit, but the bullet had not gone through. It was still in there.

"Damn!" I snapped.

Jerri came over with the whisky and I said, "Pour it on the wounds."

As she did that both waves of pain hit me at once. The shock wore off and I could feel the pain being caused by that hot slug of lead that was in my arm, as well as the burning caused by the alcohol.

"Give me some of that," I said, grabbing the bottle as the sweat broke out on my brow. I swallowed a good portion of the fiery liquor, then poured some more on the wound.

"Get something to wrap around it," I told her.

After a few moments my arm was tightly bound, which I hoped would keep the bleeding down to a minimum. There was no time to root around in there for the bullet. It would have to wait until later —if there was a later.

"Get back to the window," I said to her, and I got back to my front window. I looked out at the body of Stitch McCord, wondering if taking a slug in the arm was worth cutting Bull Martin's number by one. McCord had not been as good as his rep, which meant that it wasn't worth it. Not a damn bit!

Chapter Forty-nine

After that things got so quiet I was in danger of falling asleep. My wound, coupled with the bottle of whisky I'd finished, was making my eyes feel very heavy. It was when Jerri fired a shot through her window that I jerked awake, shouting, "What the hell?"

"They're trying to move around back, Clint," she said.

"Well, discourage them, damn it!"

Outside I heard more shots, and figured some of them were also trying to work their way down the street. It wouldn't be long before they circled the whole street. That would force Bat to fire one way and Wyatt the other, destroying any chance we had of getting them in a crossfire.

I moved to the door where I could see better and sure enough, I saw a few men coming down the street from the other way. I fired a couple of shots to discourage them and to alert Wyatt and Bat, if they hadn't already spotted them. Then I backed away from the door and went back to the window.

"Your Pa's a tactician," I said aloud, but Jerri either didn't hear me, or didn't care to comment.

When she fired a couple of more shots, I wondered if she were firing high, or attempting accuracy. If she were firing over their heads and they realized it at any point, they'd simply rush us from the back, and they'd have us.

My fears were realized when she whispered, "Damn you."

"Jerri?"

"He won't stop coming," she said in a dull voice.

I walked halfway across the room to her, then stopped and said, "Is it one of your brothers?"

She shook her head and said, "No."

"Then kill the sonofabitch!" I snapped. "That'll stop him!"

She leveled her gun, hesitated a moment, then squeezed off a shot that was followed by a man's cry.

"Good girl. That'll discourage them."

"Yeah," she replied dully, and broke her gun open to reload. I decided to simply leave her be and get back to my own window.

They finally got smart and started moving down the street from both directions at the same time. I could hear Bat and Wyatt firing, probably in opposite directions. I began to fire, alternating my direction of fire. I saw one man spin and fall. I didn't know which one of us hit him, but I pumped a round into his fallen body, just to be sure. With him, Stitch, and the man Jerri had shot, their number was down to eight. The odds were getting better.

I wondered where Bull Martin was. If I could get to him, that might put a stop to the whole thing, but finding him meant going out on the street again. My left arm had stiffened, which would badly hamper my movements out there. I shelved that idea for the moment.

How long before they simply rush us? I wondered.

Another volley of shots drew my attention, and as I looked up at Wyatt I saw him drop from sight.

"Shit!" I shouted.

"What happened?" Jerri asked.

"Wyatt's been hit."

"How bad?"

"I can't tell."

I kept watching for him to get up, but he didn't, and after a few moments I stopped watching. I wondered about Bat. For all I knew he could have been hit, too. They could both be dead, leaving just Jerri and me.

As if to prove me wrong I heard Bat firing a few shots down into the street. He could still have been hit, but he was able to rain some lead down on their heads, and that was what counted.

"How long can we keep this up?" Jerri asked.

"As long as we possibly can, Jerri," I replied.

"It's hopeless," she said, and I didn't reply. I was too busy firing. When the hammer of my rifle fell with a dull click, I discarded it and took out my revolver. I fired three quick shots and then withdrew in time to avoid a hail of bullets that struck all about the window. I heard a gasp of pain from behind me, and turned quickly.

There was a spot of blossoming redness on Jerri's back, high on the right side, and she had fallen against the wall. One of those deadly slugs had come through the window and found its mark in her back.

"Jerri!" I shouted.

"Clint," she called back, so weakly I could barely hear her.

I got up to go to her and another volley hit from directly across the street. I threw myself flat, shouting to her at the same time.

She made the fatal mistake of pushing herself off the wall to her feet, and turning towards me, her face wracked with pain. Another slug struck her between those beautiful breasts and she was thrown violently against the wall. Her eyes stared at me in total surprise, then they went vacant, and she fell.

"Oh, Goddamn," I whispered.

Chapter Fifty

Lying there on the floor, staring at her fallen body, I was dimly aware that the frequency of shots from outside had increased drastically, and I pushed myself painfully off the floor and scrambled over to the door.

The men directly across the street from me, who had fired the volley that had killed Jerri, were firing again, but up the street, where their own men should have been. Puzzled, I pushed myself out the door to see who they were firing at, and who was firing at them. Whoever it was, they were firing accurately, because as I watched one, two, and then the third man fell to the ground and didn't move again.

One of them I recognized as Ben Martin. It would be ironic if he had been the one who fired that last shot that had killed his sister.

There were three men on horseback down the street, firing in all directions. They were not part of Bull Martin's bunch. Bat was firing from the roof, and I started adding my own lead to the party.

Bull Martin's forces were being routed—worse for them, they were being slaughtered. The unexpected appearance of the three men on horses had caught them flatfooted and unawares.

I turned my attention to the other direction and saw Wes and Jim Martin approaching from that side. Their faces betrayed their surprise, and then their fear. A shot from Bat's rifle sent Wes spinning to the ground. Jim looked at his brother, then at me. He opened his mouth to say something, and I put a bullet in it. He fell atop his brother.

"Clint!" I heard someone shout. I looked across the street and my stomach jumped as I realized it was Wyatt, down on street level now. His shirtfront was covered with blood as he fired a round past me. I turned in time to see Beau Martin clutch his chest and fall. He had apparently climbed through the rear window of the hotel, and then come out the front door. Had Wyatt not shot him, he would have shot me in the back.

When he fell to the ground with an audible thump, it was the last sound we heard for a few moments.

The shooting was over.

Then someone yelled, "Wyatt!"

Two of the three men who had rode in ran towards Wyatt and caught him before he could fall. I knew then that they were Wyatt's brothers, Morgan and Virgil.

I turned to see the third man come walking towards me, his gun in his hand, but pointing at the ground. At that moment, Bat walked out of the hotel, rifle in hand, bleeding from a gash over his right eye.

"Billy!" the man cried upon seeing Bat, and he ran to him and embraced him.

This had to be Bat's brother, Ed.

While the brothers assured each other that they were fine, I searched the streets for Bull Martin.

He was nowhere to be found.

The Earp brothers walked Wyatt across to us and we all congregated in front of the hotel.

"Wyatt, how bad?" I asked.

"Creased my neck," he said, showing me the gash on the right side of his neck. "It bled worse than it is."

"Bat?" I said, turning to the Mastersons.

"Just a gash over my eye, from a chunk of flying wood, not lead. How about you?"

"We get this piece of lead out of me, I'll be fine, but there's something else I have to do first."

"What's that?" Morgan Earp asked. The Earps were all the same, tall and slim, obviously brothers. Bat's brother Ed was slighter than him, but again, they were obviously kin.

"Bull Martin," I said. "I want him."

"What about Jerri?" Wyatt asked.

"She's inside," Bat said, sadly.

"She's dead, Wyatt. Killed by one of her own brothers, I think, but actually killed by her father, Bull, who started this whole thing because he'd lost one son. Now he's got nothing."

I walked out into the street and shouted, "Bull Martin! I hope you're satisfied!"

There was no reply.

"Come on out, Bull," I yelled. "It's over. There'll be no more shooting."

We waited a few moments, and then we saw him. He climbed out of the empty horse trough I had been hiding behind earlier, and he held his hands out away from his body. He didn't have a gun.

"Come and look at your family, Bull," I told him.

He walked down the street with a stoic expression on his face. He stopped near us and looked at the bodies of his sons impassively.

"Where's Jerri?" he asked.

"Inside," I replied.

He looked at me and said, "You want to finish the job?"

I looked at the Earps, the Mastersons, the dead Martins, and then at Bull Martin.

"I'm too tired, Bull, and you're not worth the effort."

He stared at me arrogantly for a long moment, then brushed past me and went into the hotel to see Jerri.

"This certainly turned out to be a family affair, didn't it?" I asked.

I suddenly felt very alone in the world.

"We better get you fellas tended to," Ed Masterson said.

"Why not?" I replied. "No sense going through all of this just to bleed to death."

We all entered the hotel with me in the lead, and I listened with half an ear as Morgan and Virgil Earp were saying how they had hooked up with Ed Masterson in Zuni Flats.

When we got inside we saw Bull Martin kneeling down next to the body of his daughter, and all talking stopped out of respect for the dead, and for the man who was mourning for his dead.

As Bull stood up I became aware that I was still holding my gun in my hand. I was about to put it away when he turned to us with a *leer* and a mad glint in his eye and said, "She was some damn good lay."

"You bastard!" I shouted, and instead of putting my gun away, I pulled the trigger.

GREAT BOOKS

E-BOOKS

AUDIOBOOKS

& MORE

Visit us today

www.speakingvolumes.us